KUDZU'S ENORMOUS NEW LIFE

KUDZU'S ENORMOUS NEW LIFE

Sidney Thompson

atmosphere press

Published by Atmosphere Press

Cover design and illustrations by Sarah Gledhill

atmospherepress.com

Contents

CHAPTER 1

Life on the Spectrum

Autumn had finally arrived at the farm, which lay in a great valley where the Mississippi River once flowed hundreds of years ago. Where alligators once swam and sunned themselves on the river's muddy banks. Where pelicans once nested in great numbers, who would glide on enormous wings just above the water's surface and scoop up meals of fish in their enormous beaks. But hunters have long since killed all the alligators, the pelicans have forever flown away, and the river gradually changed its course, creeping little by little westward, now a day's bicycle ride away.

What remained hundreds of years later in the valley was the river's old bed, its dark, rich, fertile soil, perfect for all flowers and trees and plants in a garden to grow healthy in. And it was perfect for digging and sleeping soundly in. In fact, to some who lived on the farm in this ancient river valley, it was the softest, the sweetest, the most comfortable, most delightful dirt in the whole wide wonderfully dirty world.

And there was no better time to enjoy the farm than in early autumn, when Mr. Weatherby's pecan and persimmon trees were full, and the nuts and ripened fruit were beginning to rain upon the ground. Now, the nights were cool but not too cool, and the days were warm but not too warm. And Mrs.

Weatherby's flowers were blossoming in every toy shape and candy color. There were cigar plants, daisies, marigolds, and goldenrods, and there were petunias, spider lilies, and painted tongues. They buzzed with thirsty bees and moths and butterflies, and with the ruby-throated hummingbirds that sometimes passed through on their migration farther southward. Autumn was a beautiful and busy season, a time of harmony and friendship. Everyone woke early and worked together each day toward the common goal of preparing for the coming hardships of winter.

Every morning, as soon as the rooster in the chicken yard perched on his favorite fence post and started to crow, Mr. and Mrs. Weatherby rose out of bed to get to work. While Mr. Weatherby dressed for chores outdoors, Mrs. Weatherby put on her robe and went into the kitchen to start breakfast. While she made her biscuits from scratch, she would glance out her window at the sun's heavenly light making her dew-moist flowers sparkle like stars. The old couple had a daughter, but she hadn't lived at home for a very long time and only visited her parents two or three times a year. Sometimes she and her husband would leave their three-year-old son with his grandparents for a few days, at most a week or two. For the rest of the time, however, there was no child or grandchild on the farm, so Mrs. Weatherby had grown to think of her flowers as her children.

Some of her flowers bloomed only in the spring, some only in the summer, and others only in the fall. She watered her flowers each and every season. She even got down on her worn-out, old knees and weeded the flowerbeds herself. And when she wasn't working to keep her flowers colorful and growing, she simply enjoyed looking at them every chance she got. She had her flowers like Mr. Weatherby had his chickens.

What Mrs. Weatherby was unable to see from her window was the life that stirred every morning below her flowers. Hidden among the thick, green, leafy stems of the daisies was a hole in the ground the size of a fifty-cent piece. And down that hole, at the end of a long tunnel, there was a nest made of grass in a small, cave-like den. Beside the nest there usually lay the remains of a late-night snack. Today what lay on the dirt floor were the broken pieces of a pecan shell and an acorn, but what was *not* there was the acorn's cap. No, in any other burrow, the acorn's hard, round cap with the pointy top would be popped off like a bottle cap and thrown aside with the other trash, but this was Kudzu's burrow. And anything was possible when Kudzu was around. He was no average chipmunk. He always made sure of that.

Kudzu had gotten in the habit lately of wearing acorn caps on his head to keep the slender space between his ears warm on cool nights. His mother had always taught him to curl up tight and place his tail between his ears. She probably didn't know about acorn caps. He knew that they looked funny on him. Chipmunks aren't supposed to wear hats! And he felt funny wearing them, but he liked to laugh at himself at times. His father had always said if you couldn't enjoy laughing at yourself, then you probably couldn't enjoy much of anything else. Kudzu agreed. That was why, when he uncurled himself out of his sleeping position this morning, he was wearing a night cap that only an oak tree can make.

He stretched out his arms, opened his big, sleepy brown eyes, and yawned in a big breath of fresh October air. "Ahhh!" he said to himself with a smile. He wondered, "Can life get any better than this?"

As if something were answering his question, as if the world itself were telling him that life can only get worse before it can get better, the ground began to shake. Kudzu raised his nose into the air and twitched his whiskers, but all he could smell was the dirt sprinkling down around him. The ground rumbled louder and louder and began to shake even greater, making Kudzu's cap slide off his head and roll away.

"Oh, no!" Kudzu said to himself. It finally occurred to him what was happening. This was an earthquake!

Kudzu jumped to his hind feet and started to dart for the emergency tunnel behind his nest, which he had dug in case a snake ever decided to slither in after him. But before he could move, the ceiling of his dirt home crumbled apart, and suddenly the sun was shining down on him. Kudzu was shocked. His bedroom had never had a window before. He had never considered it even possible. Then the sun vanished, as if behind an enormous dark cloud, and what appeared in its place above Kudzu was larger and more frightening than any snake he'd ever seen or any hawk he'd ever heard stories about. What hovered over Kudzu was perhaps the chipmunk's most-feared enemy: a dog!

And this dog was not just any dog. It was no teary-eyed toy poodle. No shivering, little Chihuahua. This was a seventy-pound German shepherd, solid black, with claws ten times larger than Kudzu's and with teeth that were longer and sharper than fence nails.

The dog stopped pawing at the dirt and lowered his enormous head, with ears that stood straight up just like Kudzu's. Then with his brown eyes, the dog looked at Kudzu, and Kudzu looked back at him. For a moment, as they stared at one another, neither of them breathed or blinked their eyes or made a sound. It was as if the dog was stunned to see Kudzu as much as Kudzu was to see him. Kudzu had never come face to face with a dog before, and maybe this was the dog's first time meeting a chipmunk. Maybe, thought Kudzu, a dog could be scared off by a chipmunk's impressive bark.

At the beginning of spring earlier this year, when Kudzu first moved away from his childhood home to build his own home and his own life, he tried to make friends by making trouble. He would sneak up behind a frog or a mole or a roly-poly and would bark as loud as he could. He thought scaring everybody on the farm was fun until he barked once at a pair of mourning doves who were on their honeymoon. The doves were busy feeding each other, so they didn't notice Kudzu creeping up. When Kudzu was about an inch away from them, he let out the best bark of his life. The doves fainted right there on the spot. Kudzu hadn't barked at anybody since. But now his home—the first one of his own making—was at stake. He had to do something.

Kudzu took the deepest breath he'd ever taken, then raised his fists. "Chip! Chip! Chip!" he barked.

The dog cocked his head sideways. Maybe he couldn't believe such a loud bark could come out of such a small creature. But when the shepherd parted his lips, it seemed to Kudzu that the dog was grinning at him. Then, in an instant, the dog's enormous mouth had stretched open and was coming to snatch Kudzu up.

Kudzu leaped off his bed and, in the same motion, turned and dove into his escape tunnel. A split second later, he heard the dog's jaws and teeth snap shut behind him.

Kudzu scurried to the opposite end of the tunnel and was already digging out the plug to his secret entrance when he heard Mrs. Weatherby's booming voice.

"Get away from there! Get! Get!" she hollered.

Kudzu scratched away the dirt and poked his head out of the ground.

Mrs. Weatherby was shaking a rolling pin at the shepherd as he ran away. She turned and looked at her flowerbed. Around the main entrance to Kudzu's burrow, the dog had stomped the life out of the daisies. Some were dug out of the ground and lay broken on the grass. The scattered yellow and white blossoms now looked like splattered eggs.

"Oh, no, my poor daisies!" she said with a voice full of sorrow. Kudzu looked again at what the dog had done, and he felt sorry for them, and for Mrs. Weatherby. He had grown to think of her over time as his friend, and now he knew he had been correct. He could count on her to protect him and his burrow, his life and his world.

Mrs. Weatherby shook her head and went back inside the house. Kudzu shook his head, too, then began the daylong task of building a new burrow.

CHAPTER 2

Owen

At noon, it was as if the two friends had agreed to take a break at the same time from all their work in the flowerbed. Mrs. Weatherby had filled in the hole that the dog had made, then had replanted all the daisies that could be replanted and had given them a long drink of water. She had worked at a slow but steady pace, and so had Kudzu. He had already dug out a tunnel underneath the spider lilies and had carved out a big, roomy den. He had carried the dirt out of his burrow by packing it into his cheeks and spitting it out above ground. That was the worst part of building a home. The taste of the dirt wasn't bad. Not here on this farm. But even the best-tasting dirt will stick to your mouth and make you gag.

Kudzu also had made a nice, soft nest of grass and moss that his mother would've been proud of. He hadn't started on his escape tunnel yet, but he had built a storage room for his winter nuts, which were still stored at his old burrow. He would get them later. First, he needed to rest. It was lunchtime, but he wasn't hungry. In fact, he had eaten while he worked. Whenever he had come upon an earthworm or a grub worm during his digging, he stopped to eat it before moving on. And thanks to Mrs. Weatherby and her hose water, he wasn't thirsty, and his mouth wasn't dry or gritty anymore from dirt. But he was tired, so he lay down on his new bed and shut his eyes.

To Kudzu, life in a flowerbed was paradise. Everything he needed was right there. Whenever he was thirsty, there was Mrs. Weatherby and her hose, like clockwork. And the flowers not only looked pretty, smelled sweet, and offered him shade from the sun, but also attracted many animals that usually became either his food or his friends. None was a close friend or best friend yet, not someone he could tell secrets to or share his burrow with, but he had reason to hope it would one day happen. In the meantime, he couldn't imagine living anywhere else. His parents would be so proud of him.

What he could imagine, what he was now imagining in his sleep, was that he was walking into the mysterious woods that lay on the edge of the farm. From the outside, the trees were as beautiful in color as any flower, but inside the woods, it was dark—so dark that he could see nothing in front of him. He had to use only his sense of smell to lead him to the tallest tree in the woods, the only pine tree among oak, ash, maple, hickory, and sweetgum. And with his nose, he tracked the pine tree down, and he did not trip or bump into anything on his way there. Then up he climbed. The tree seemed to go up forever, yet Kudzu never tired. When he finally reached the top, the highest branch of the tallest tree, he could see for the first time in his life the Mississippi River, the widest and longest river in all of America. It flowed by in the distance like a calm and harmless snake, shining silver in the sun.

He was enjoying his new burrow, his new bed, and one of his old, favorite dreams when the ground around him began to tremble. In his dream, Kudzu hung onto the branch, but the tree began to shake so badly that it started to sway from side to side, and he could not hang on any longer. He had to let go, and when he did, he dropped. But he never reached the ground. He kept falling and falling through space, and even though he was in the air, he felt the ground shake—just as he had that morning. That was when he realized that he was not falling. That he was not in the woods. That he was in the flowerbed, and the dog was back!

His eyes shot open, he hopped to his feet, and without wasting any time, Kudzu dove for his escape tunnel. He had forgotten, however, that he hadn't made his escape tunnel yet, so Kudzu ended up landing on his head. He didn't hurt himself, but he had to sit down and hold onto his bed because his room was spinning. If only he'd been wearing an acorn hat!

He was afraid the end was near now. His ceiling was beginning to crumble down on top of him. Then, just as suddenly as the terror had started, it stopped.

"Get out of there!" he heard Mrs. Weatherby shout. For the second time, she had come to Kudzu's rescue.

Kudzu shook the dirt off his head and shoulders and ran through the tunnel. Although he raised his head high enough for only one of his eyes to peek out, he couldn't believe what that one eye saw. The wonderful yellow-and-green striped spider lilies around the opening of his new burrow had been clawed out of the ground. Mrs. Weatherby was standing a good distance away with her head down and her hands on her hips.

Mr. Weatherby appeared from around the backside of the house, from the direction of the toolshed. He wore gloves, and stepping in his long shadow was a brown-haired boy dragging a rake. The boy resembled Mr. Weatherby's grandson, Owen, a boy who would only say "no" the last time Kudzu had seen him—that one word and nothing else, no matter how many times the Weatherbys had asked and begged and pleaded for more. He was a boy who they said was on the spectrum, was special that way, but if he was always walking on a spectrum, which was another way of saying *rainbow*, no one saw it. Maybe, Kudzu wondered, the boy grunted and screamed a lot because he didn't see it either, which would be disappointing and really confusing. He could no doubt scream. He could scream like a blue jay—no, like a cat. No, like both of them screaming at once!

But this boy was a little taller than Owen, the top of his head meeting Mr. Weatherby's belt. He took bigger steps, too, and was a little faster and steadier on his feet than Kudzu remembered Owen to be. Then Kudzu recognized the serious yet joyful "there's work to be done and I'm doing it" twinkle about the boy's big chipmunk-like eyes and knew this boy had to be Owen. Maybe that was the sign of the spectrum—that twinkle that adult humans saw a different way, for some reason as something he stood on or sat on, like shoulders, while others, like Kudzu, saw it within him and shining out.

"Look," Mrs. Weatherby said with great sadness. She pointed at the mess in the flowerbed. "And after I spent all day making it right again!"

Mr. Weatherby removed his gloves as he walked up to Mrs. Weatherby. He placed a hand on her shoulder. "I'll take care of it," he told her.

Owen let the rake handle fall from his hands and reached down to pick up one of the strewn flowers. "Er," he said.

Mr. Weatherby bent down to the boy. "That's a flower," he said, and gently removed the flower from the boy's hand and laid it down on the unpacked earth. "Don't touch. No touch, okay, Owen? We'll plant it back in the ground in a bit, you and me, okay?"

"Uh-huh," he said, looking almost mad.

Mr. Weatherby smiled and patted the boy on the head. "Can you say *flower*?"

"Er," Owen said with a smile.

Mr. Weatherby bit down on his bottom lip and leaned in closer to Owen. "*Flower*," he said, really stretching the word out by blowing lots of air through his teeth and rounding his tongue into a frog-like thing.

"Noooo!" Owen hollered. He stomped and shook his hands. Kudzu covered his ears with his paws, expecting Owen to scream like only he could, but this time he didn't.

"It's okay, Owen," Mr. Weatherby said, rubbing the boy's back and calming him. He patted Owen again on the head and stood up. He looked at Mrs. Weatherby, so Kudzu looked at her, but Mrs. Weatherby simply shrugged her shoulders.

"Huh," Kudzu said to himself as he uncovered his ears. He'd never realized how similar human children were to any other misunderstood animal. He felt bad for the boy, who had said more than his grandparents could hear or understand.

"Something's going to have to be done about that dog," Mrs. Weatherby said.

"Ga," Owen said.

Unaware of what Owen had said, Mr. Weatherby continued looking at Mrs. Weatherby, and she continued looking at him. Then Mr. Weatherby nodded. "Something will be," he said. "I'll see to it."

Well, that was all Kudzu needed to hear. Mr. Weatherby was a man of his word. If he said something would be done about that dog, that he'd see to it, then Kudzu and Mrs. Weatherby could count on him doing exactly that. Kudzu worried no more. Instead, what Kudzu did was get back to work.

While Mr. Weatherby and Owen shoveled and spooned the dirt back into the flowerbed for Mrs. Weatherby and replanted all of her spider lilies that could be replanted, Kudzu dug not one but two escape tunnels. Even though Kudzu could count on Mr. Weatherby for ridding the farm of that crazed canine, he figured that he'd better prepare for the worst. Kudzu's father had taught him that good things didn't always happen when you wanted them to. In fact, he had always said that the very best things in life required enormous effort and then twice that much patience. If a chipmunk wasn't always willing to be prepared in this wild world, Kudzu's father didn't believe that one would live long enough to get anything worth wanting.

Once Kudzu had finally broken through to sunlight on the last of the two tunnels, he sat down on a rock to catch his breath. He shook out the crumbles of dirt that had fallen into his ears, and suddenly he heard a truck rumbling up the driveway. One that sounded much louder than Mr. Weatherby's old work truck. With his paw, Kudzu wiped the mud off the wet tip of his nose and watched a box-shaped truck roll near, with two men inside whom Kudzu had never seen before. They wore matching blue caps turned backward, and they were laughing, both with their windows down. The driver had a beard like a billy goat, and the passenger, who seemed much larger, had long red hair and an arm hanging out his window that made him look half-reptile, with black bands and splotches of color across his skin. And in his hand, between his fingers, he held a little white stick.

Neither Mr. Weatherby nor Mrs. Weatherby ever carried such a little white stick between their fingers, and neither did Owen, and since Kudzu hadn't spent much time around any other humans, he didn't have any idea what that little white stick was made of or used for. So he watched the red-haired half-reptile man carefully and was shocked to see him put the stick to his lips, as if he were really going to eat it. As the truck passed, the half-reptile man pulled the stick back out of his mouth, and blowing smoke, he flicked it curiously into the air as if it might fly away on its own, like a baby bird.

Kudzu watched the stick fly, tossing end over end, and he watched it come—*oh, no!*—directly at him. Kudzu leaped off his rock just before the white stick struck the rock. Sparks flew with a shower of gray flakes, and the stick bounced back into the air. Kudzu looked up and watched it turn end over end again, smoking and burning, and then drop into the fresh opening of his tunnel.

"My new home!" cried Kudzu. He scurried into the tunnel after the stick, and he had to hold his breath and squint his eyes because of the nasty smoke, the nasty smell, which was worse even than the smell of a stink bug! And it made him feel a little dizzy, too. He had to get this weird fire stick out of his burrow immediately. He clamped his teeth around the end that wasn't burning, which was strangely soft and spongy like a caterpillar's cocoon, and he walked backwards, dragging the stick behind him until he was finally above ground again. Then, as he rubbed his eyes and coughed, he kicked dirt on the stick until it was no longer burning and no longer in sight, totally buried and hopefully forgotten.

"Whew!" Kudzu said to himself, relieved that the adventure was over. He looked through the spider lilies at the parked truck and at the men who were now standing on the Weatherbys' porch and knocking on their door. He shook his head in disbelief. Why in the world would they launch such a deadly weapon upon innocent bystanders? Those men were worse than fire ants, worse than wasps, worse than anything Kudzu had ever seen in his young life.

Mrs. Weatherby came to the door, and before long, the men returned to the truck, opened the rear doors, and started carrying boxes into the house. Apparently, the Weatherbys were preparing for winter the way chipmunks did, only they received their supplies by men in trucks. This reminded Kudzu of the work he had left to do.

Kudzu headed toward the hole of his old burrow. He had to begin moving all his nuts that he would need for the coming winter. If he didn't have a storage room of nuts, he'd starve to death because there would be very little food above ground for him to find. And he would freeze to death attempting to collect it. Even if somehow he could survive the cold, he would still be in danger of being hunted by the many starving animals that roamed constantly over ice and snow. No, it was best for Kudzu to hibernate all winter long in the warmth of his burrow, where he could safely sleep and eat until spring.

When Kudzu had emptied his last mouthful of nuts into his new storage room, he stumbled into his bedroom—but not before putting on his protective headgear. With an acorn cap sitting crown-like on his head, he opened his arms, like a kind king, and dropped chest-first into his nest. Sleep fell upon him quickly. It was heavy and long, but it was dreamless.

CHAPTER 3

Victoria

When Kudzu woke the following morning, later than he normally woke, he felt slow, as though he hadn't slept much at all.

As he stretched the sore muscles of his arms and legs that morning, Kudzu realized that he was starving, not simply hungry but *starving*. All of the hard work he'd done yesterday had caught up with him. A few pecans would make him feel like new, though. He always felt better after breakfast.

Once Kudzu had bathed himself, had brushed his tail and had straightened his cap, he went up one flight to ground level.

"Ahhh," he said happily to himself. Life was back to normal. The flowers were in the ground where they were supposed to be. Bees and moths and butterflies were feeding on the flowers once again. And the dog was nowhere to be seen. Mr. Weatherby was true to his word.

"I suppose you're hungry, Kudzu." These words came to him from a high, thin voice that he recognized.

Kudzu looked up, and there she was, perched on a purple petunia, with her black-and-orange wings waving open and closed as gently and as quietly as Kudzu's own lungs were breathing in and out.

Kudzu smiled. "Good morning, Victoria."

"No, good is not good enough, Kudzu. I should say *exquisite*," she told him.

"*Exquisite*?" said Kudzu. Monarch butterflies were always using complicated words that Kudzu didn't understand, and Victoria was no exception. He didn't mind, of course. How could he ever grow smarter if his vocabulary never grew bigger? It didn't seem possible to Kudzu's mother and father, and it didn't seem possible to Kudzu.

"*Exquisite*," said Victoria, "is a word to describe something most delicate and lovely, of the finest order."

"Like your wings?" asked Kudzu.

"There's nothing more exquisite than a butterfly's wings, indeed," she agreed. "Now," she said, which was what Victoria always said before changing the subject. She lofted herself into the air and floated to a spider lily blossom closer to Kudzu. "Mr. Weatherby has already been out gathering pecans this morning, and there are no more under the trees for you. He took them all. I saw him. But Mr. Weatherby has been kind enough to leave his late-rising chipmunk a meal."

Kudzu's wide eyes grew wider. He had no idea that Mr. Weatherby had ever given him a single thought. "Really? Are you sure?" he asked Victoria.

"Would Mr. Weatherby have left pecans in a nice, little basket on the ground for anyone else?" Her antennae pointed in the direction of the pecan-tree orchard. "See for yourself," she told him. She then turned to the flower in front of her and unrolled the long straw of her coiled proboscis. She stuck it down into the flower and began to suck the sweet nectar into her mouth.

Kudzu ducked underneath the surrounding leaves and stems of the flowers and crossed the flowerbed in the direction of the pecan trees. When he reached the other side, he saw what Victoria had seen. On the lawn sat a box-shaped basket that was as silver as the Mississippi River had been in his dreams. And inside the basket, at the far end of the opening on a tiny table, there were four pecan halves. The sight of the shelled and cleaned meat sitting there waiting for him made Kudzu's tail wag. The Weatherbys had remembered their friendly chipmunk, who caused no trouble for anyone—unlike that stray dog.

Happy to be so loved, Kudzu ran inside the box-shaped basket to eat his breakfast. His front teeth clicked excitedly together as he picked up the largest nut off the table, but as soon as he did, he heard a clicking sound that his teeth hadn't made. The sound came from behind him, so he turned around and saw a door come falling down over the entrance to the basket.

Kudzu dropped the pecan and ran to the door, but he couldn't lift it up. He scurried along all sides of the silver-wire basket, looking for another way out. But there wasn't one. He was trapped!

Kudzu yelled for help, and Victoria soon fluttered into view. She floated down in front of Kudzu, on the other side of the cage bars, and grinned at him.

"Well," said Victoria, "aren't you in a fix!"

"What did I ever do to you?" asked Kudzu. "Why did you trick me?"

"Maybe now," said Victoria, "you'll stay away from my flowers." Then with a flash of her wings, she was gone, lifted away, back to the flowers.

"But I didn't hurt your flowers," yelled Kudzu. "That was the dog, not me! The dog!"

Kudzu turned his attention to the trap door again. With all his weight, he tried to lift it open, tried to push it open, tried to pull it open and bite it open and kick it open, but nothing worked. Then he heard and saw Mr. Weatherby and Owen walking his way, coming from the direction of the chicken coop. Mr. Weatherby was carrying a tin bucket with one hand and holding Owen's hand with the other. And then Mr. Weatherby suddenly stopped. He appeared to see Kudzu. He appeared to be looking directly at him.

Kudzu backed up and hid underneath the table of pecan halves. He watched Mr. Weatherby and then Owen step closer. Mr. Weatherby set his bucket on the ground and lowered his face to the cage.

"Look, Owen," he said.

Owen pressed his face closer, his brown eyes becoming the fattest of acorns, his brown hair looking thick as a cap. His sweet smile grew wide, showing Kudzu his teeth, which were square, anything but sharp, but they were teeth so they were large enough and frightening enough.

"Trying to keep the fox out of the chicken coop is enough for this old man," said Mr. Weatherby. "Mama and I don't need you to worry us, too, little chipmunk." He studied Kudzu for a moment with flat blue eyes, like circles of sky.

Kudzu tried his best to smile, to change Mr. Weatherby's mind or heart, but was too nervous, shaking too much, to make a real one.

"That's a chipmunk, Owen," Mr. Weatherby said. "*Chipmunk.*"

"Ka," Owen said.

Mr. Weatherby arched his eyebrows at Kudzu. "You're a cute thing, though. I hate to have to kill you."

Kudzu's mouth dropped open. "But, Mr. Weatherby, we're friends," he said. But Mr. Weatherby's ears couldn't hear all sounds; they couldn't hear what Kudzu could. So to Mr. Weatherby, Kudzu had said, "Bamiwitterfred." Only nonsense.

Mr. Weatherby slowly rose to his feet and brushed off his overalls.

"Ends," smiled Owen.

Kudzu gasped. "You hear me? You do hear me? You really hear me and understand? You'll be my friend?"

Owen laughed.

Mr. Weatherby picked up his bucket of eggs. "Come on, Owen," he said. "Let's get you inside. There are things you don't need to see." He took Owen's hand, but Owen squealed about leaving and pulled away from him.

"Ka!" he said.

"Let's see what your grandma's cooking up," Mr. Weatherby said. "Let's go see Grandma. Want to?" He reached again for Owen's hand, and they continued walking toward the house.

Kudzu hurried out from under the table. He didn't have much time, but he didn't know what to do. He wanted to cry, but he wouldn't let himself. He had to stay calm. He couldn't panic. If he decided to, if he truly wanted to badly enough, he could think his way out of this. If he put his best effort into getting out.

He took a deep breath and worked his brain as fast and as hard as it would go. Just as he trusted would happen, an idea came to him. Maybe he could make the trap work in reverse. Maybe if he put the pecan back on the table and took it off again, then the door would go back up. But what happened next, what he saw when he turned around, made him forget that idea forever.

The German shepherd had reappeared, and he was staring into the cage with mad-dog eyes. Kudzu didn't know what to do now. Either way, if he escaped or if he didn't, Kudzu would die.

"Come out of there," the dog told him. Then the dog slapped his paw against the side of the cage, causing Kudzu to lose his balance and fall back on his bottom. The dog laughed at Kudzu and pawed again at the cage, this time with more force, and the cage tilted over. But it didn't stop there. The cage kept turning, rolling down the hill toward the pecan orchard, and the dog hopped after it. Kudzu was tossed around inside, landing on his head and bottom, on his head and bottom, over and over again. It was a good thing he remembered today to wear his acorn cap!

When the cage finally came to rest at the base of the hill, Kudzu found himself lying upside down in the upside-down cage. Dizzy, Kudzu slowly crawled to his four feet. Swaying as he stood and gazing at a square space of cageless air, he realized that in the tumble, the trap door had fallen open. He lifted a foot to take the first step of his escape, but the dog was faster, leaping suddenly in front of the cage and blocking the opening with his mouth. Panting and grinning, with his long, pink tongue dangling out over mountains of teeth, the dog looked devilish.

"Please," said Kudzu, but before he could finish, the dog turned away, as if he'd seen something frightening. Kudzu looked over his shoulder and saw Mr. Weatherby hurrying down the hill with a garden hoe.

The shepherd looked at Kudzu. "I'll catch you later," he said, then darted away.

"I'll get you!" shouted Mr. Weatherby. He swung the blade of the hoe at the dog and struck him across his chest. The dog yelped, but kept running, leaping away on his long, rabbit-like legs.

Kudzu put his hands on his head in disbelief. He'd never seen Mr. Weatherby hurt anyone for anything. And Victoria had never lied to him before. In one day, Kudzu's whole world had turned upside down. The dog had made everybody on the farm as crazy as he was and turn against each other. And now Kudzu was going to have to run for his life because Mr. Weatherby was jogging toward the cage with his hoe held high, coming for him!

Kudzu leaped out of the cage and began to zig-zag through the grass. Luckily, he was faster than Mr. Weatherby, but Kudzu had no place to go. He only knew that he had to keep moving and missing the swings of Mr. Weatherby's hoe. So Kudzu ran and kept running, going farther across the farm than he'd ever gone before. Once the pecan orchard was behind him and Mr. Weatherby was even farther behind him, he didn't stop. And he wouldn't stop. Not until he'd made it to the other side of the pasture, past the open range of a hawk's eye.

Kudzu now had a goal in mind. He headed for the woods that lay at the edge of the farm, just in front of him. The trees burst with red leaves, looking like flames of fire. And in the fire and around the fire, there were bunches and bunches of bright yellow leaves, which appeared to hover in the trees like flocks of goldfinches. Until now, Kudzu had only thought of the woods as a dark and strange, distant place where the night animals lived. A place that had appeared in his dreams since the spring, when he'd first laid eyes on its enormous mystery. Now, the mystery had grown even greater. It was a fire that didn't burn, yet he knew all the same that its exquisite beauty wouldn't last forever.

CHAPTER 4

Ophelia

Some days just don't feel like other days. Sometimes a day feels so different that it should have its very own name. It's not one that comes around every week or even as often as once a year. Such a day feels like it belongs to you and nobody else, and that's because it does.

Kudzu was having one of those days today. It wasn't half over yet, but already so much had happened to him that he expected everything would start feeling different to him now, including himself. As Kudzu made his frightening first step into the foreign world of the woods, he realized what today really was. Today was the beginning of a new life. And he prayed it would be a long one.

No matter how tenderly Kudzu planted his weight as he crept forward, the thick carpet of leaves would crackle beneath him. So, after taking a few steps, he stopped and rose up on his hind legs. He stood very still and listened for sounds that weren't his. But he heard nothing—nothing except the wind above, whispering through the leaves. He looked in every direction, but seeing nothing he hadn't already seen, he lowered to all fours and continued on.

Predators in the woods could hide anywhere, unlike in a burrow, so his eyes were in constant motion for anything that moved or could move. He studied the trees especially. Anything could be waiting to drop on him from a branch, or to fly at him from a knothole, or to spring at him from behind a tree trunk. And there were so many trees—in front of him, to his right and to his left, and now behind him, too.

Kudzu had gone about ten feet into the woods when he picked up the scent of a possum that had passed by not long ago. Possums were known to be friendly to chipmunks, and since Kudzu desperately needed a friend, he followed the scent.

A possum's scent could not be mistaken for any other odor. Kudzu would've described it as a cross between a wet mole and a fig. Kudzu tracked this scent deep into the woods to a fallen tree. And when he hopped on top of the tree and looked down on the other side, he found the possum. It was a female possum, perhaps his mother's age, curled up in a lifeless gray heap with a snarl across her pale face. Her eyes were shut, but Kudzu could tell she wasn't sleeping. Not with her front feet clenched into fists and her tongue hanging out of her mouth.

Kudzu cleared his throat. "Hello?" he said. "Ma'am?" He hopped off the log to examine her closer. She didn't appear to be breathing at all. "Excuse me," he said, "are you all right?"

The possum peeked at him from one eye. Then it opened wider, as though she were relaxing, and her tongue slipped back into her mouth.

"You chipmunks have big feet, you know that?" she said. "You sounded much bigger than you are."

Kudzu looked down. He did have pretty big feet. "I'm

sorry, I didn't mean to scare you," he said. Then he smiled. "I've never seen a possum playing possum before."

"And you still haven't," she told him. "Dear, what you've seen is an opossum playing opossum. I'm not a *possum*. I'm an *opossum*! Please, *please* get it right, son." She stuck her hind legs into the air and spread her five-fingered feet so that Kudzu could see them plainly. "We have opposable thumbs, like humans." She wiggled her long, crooked thumbs, then she began touching the tips of her fingers with her opposable thumbs.

Kudzu looked at his own feet and tried to do the same but couldn't. He couldn't touch even one of his fingers, or toes, with his stubby, little thumbs.

"No need to waste your time," said the opossum. "Only humans and opossums can do it—and maybe a few others, I don't know. But not many others and certainly not a chipmunk." She lowered her legs and turned over. "If I wanted to, I could grip a pencil in my hand—that's how special my opposable thumbs are, and that's how special opossums are." She sat back with her bald, snake-looking tail propping herself up. "A *possum* would not be very special. It would have *posable* thumbs and have a name like *Phelia*. But I'm an opossum, with opposable thumbs, so my name is Ophelia."

Kudzu nodded his head. "Nice to meet you, Ophelia. I'm Kudzu."

"Look, little one," Ophelia said, "I'd love to stay and chat with you, but I'm starving." She patted her belly, but she seemed stuffed already. "I've got six mouths to feed besides my own."

"You do? Where?" asked Kudzu.

Ophelia smiled. "You don't know a thing about opossums, do you?"

Kudzu shook his head. He knew about plants, flowers especially, and about worms and soil, but not about much else. Life had been easy for him for a long time. Maybe too easy, he was realizing.

Ophelia motioned with one of her fingers for him to step closer. "I want you to see something," she said, but when she placed her finger inside her belly, Kudzu stayed where he was. He was afraid she might pull out her insides and show them to him.

"I won't hurt you," she said, but Kudzu shook his head.

"I can see from here," he told her, but he was already prepared to cover his eyes.

"But I want you to see my pouch," said Ophelia. "I'm a marsupial, and you should know what a marsupial's pouch looks like. Not even a human has a pouch." Then with the finger that appeared to be still inside her belly, she pulled open a fur-lined pocket that was attached to her belly.

Without thinking about stepping forward, Kudzu simply stepped forward, attracted by the mystery of this new life. And what he saw when he walked closer and looked inside Ophelia's pouch were six sleeping baby opossums. They were as pink and hairless as their mother's tail. They weren't much bigger than baby chipmunks.

"How old are they?" asked Kudzu.

Ophelia closed her pouch. "Eight weeks."

"Wow," said Kudzu. He raised his head and smiled at Ophelia. "I wish I had a pouch."

"But you do," said Ophelia. "You have two of them."

"I do?" Kudzu scratched his head.

Ophelia reached out and touched his cheeks.

"Oh, they don't count," Kudzu said.

"Of course they do." She lowered her head so that her eyes were even with Kudzu's. "How many acorns can you carry in each of your cheeks?"

Kudzu thought for a moment. "Usually three," he said.

"Well, see!" said Ophelia. "You can carry a total of six acorns in your two pouches, just like I'm carrying six baby opossums in my one pouch. You might not be able to birth any young'uns and carry them in your pouches, like a marsupial can, but you do have pouches, Kudzu. And that makes you special."

Kudzu grinned. He hadn't thought of himself as having anything that made him special. He'd only ever thought that where he lived was special.

"This hungry litter of mine keeps me eating all the time, day and night," said Ophelia, "but look at me." She held her arms out to the side. "Look how skinny I am. I'll never fatten up for winter." She dropped to all fours. "It was nice meeting you, Kudzu, but I better get going now. It's past my mealtime."

Kudzu wasn't hungry, but as he watched Ophelia walking away, it struck Kudzu how thirsty he was. But where would he find water?

"Ophelia," he said, and when she turned around, he asked her where he could find some water.

"You don't know?" she asked.

Kudzu felt ashamed. He shook his head. "I've always been given water," he explained. "From my mother. From the sky. From Mrs. Weatherby."

Ophelia frowned as though she were sad for him. "Are you going to be okay out here by yourself, son?"

"I think so," he said.

"Just find a snail's trail and follow it," she instructed.

"When I'm thirsty, that's what I do. If there's water around, a snail's trail will always lead you there."

Kudzu thanked his new friend for her helpful advice, but when he was alone again and searching the ground for a snail's trail, he wondered if Ophelia was actually a friend. He didn't know what the rules of friendship were. He'd moved out of his parents' burrow less than a year ago and had been living a private life ever since. Maybe friends had to meet each other on a regular basis before they could be called friends. Maybe friends had to talk to each other about the same things that they talked to themselves about in private. Maybe they had to lean toward each other and open themselves up the way flowers do to the sun. Maybe that was where he and Victoria, the monarch butterfly, had gone wrong. Maybe, just maybe, the snail who had left Kudzu this trail, which Kudzu just now had found, could be his friend, if Ophelia could not be.

Cool water and kind words—Kudzu couldn't think of a better reward after following such a horrible mess. Whenever he got lost daydreaming about having friendly company or was busy looking out for danger lurking in the woods, Kudzu would accidentally step into the snail's sticky mucous trail. And this would completely gross him out. He'd have to stop and scrape his foot against the root of a tree and rub it awhile in the dirt to get it unsticky again. Sometimes he'd almost get dizzy. Kudzu had never cared for the sticky nature of snails, but he'd always liked snails themselves. In fact, he'd always felt, in a way, kin to them, since snails hibernated during the winter months, too.

The trail took Kudzu deep into the heart of the woods before it finally ended, not at water but at the snail itself. Kudzu's big, leaf-crunching feet must have scared the snail because the snail was not out of its shell, so Kudzu announced his presence with a friendly hello. This didn't bring the snail out of hiding, so Kudzu walked up to the shell and knocked, but when he did, the sound of his knock vibrated longer than it should have. The shell sounded hollow, empty.

Kudzu leaned down, looked inside the shell, and saw what appeared only to be swirling nothingness. "Hello?" he said, and his greeting echoed back at him. Kudzu couldn't understand it. He'd never heard of a snail leaving its home. He stood up, looked around, and jumped back in fright.

On top of a broad, red mushroom knelt a praying mantis, and it was licking its lips and cleaning the sticky mucous from its spiny front legs. Its large, egg-shaped eyes gazed at Kudzu.

"A chipmunk so deep in our woods? You must be lost," the mantis said. "Maybe I can be of some assistance. Hmmm?"

Kudzu and the mantis were about the same length, unless you considered Kudzu's tail, and then Kudzu was almost twice as long. Still, Kudzu easily outweighed the frightfully skinny mantis. And though the mantis had powerful teeth and jaws, they weren't powerful enough to cut through chipmunk fur and chipmunk bone, not like how Kudzu's teeth and jaws could shred the mantis with hardly any effort. Yet Kudzu was the one who was afraid. The mantis had just eaten a harmless snail as if he had no heart and no memory, no guilt, no feelings at all.

Kudzu decided he could do without water. The woods seemed to be one enormous trap worse than the one he'd escaped from earlier that day. Kudzu was then reminded of the dog. He wondered if it lay in wait for him nearby, the way this mantis must have sat waiting for the snail.

"You haven't seen a dog come through here, have you, Mister?" asked Kudzu.

"A large one?" the mantis asked.

"Yes, that's right," said Kudzu. "A large, black one. So you've seen him?"

"Is he as black as the stripes down your back?" the mantis asked.

Kudzu looked over his shoulder at his stripes. "I suppose so," he said.

The mantis folded his front legs in front of him. "Not recently," he said. "Why, are you hoping to find a large dog as black as the stripes down your back?"

"I'm hoping to avoid him!" said Kudzu. "In fact, I'd like to find my way out of these woods and get to my mom and dad's burrow, if I can." Kudzu looked up at the purplish sky. He didn't have much time if he wanted to make it to the kudzu patch before dark. Night came surprisingly sooner to the woods than it did to the open land of the farm.

Kudzu turned back to the praying mantis and removed his acorn cap as a sign of respect. "Sir," he said, taking a step forward, "would you happen to know the way to the kudzu patch?"

"I know where several are," said the mantis. "What does yours look like?"

"Oh," smiled Kudzu, "it's a real safe place, a lovely place, where kudzu vines grow as long as telephone poles. And there are so many vines that the earth is covered with a thick, green, kudzu quilt of leaves. And there's always plenty of food and drink because juicy kudzu roots are everywhere. It's a place where digging is easy, too, because grass and weeds can't grow there. Nothing else can grow but kudzu—more and more kudzu. It's a place that gets old after a while, but for a chipmunk's first home, it's perfect." Kudzu suddenly became enormously proud of his name.

The mantis shook his head at Kudzu. "I hate to break this to you," he said, "but what you've described is every kudzu patch I've ever seen."

Kudzu's smile faded into a frown, and he set his cap back on his head.

"The nearest one is that way," the mantis said, pointing in the direction of twin maple trees flaming with orange-red leaves. "Maybe it's the one."

Kudzu stared at the maples. "Maybe," he said.

"I pray, young one," said the mantis, "that you will find

what you're looking for and not what you aren't. Be alert. This is a dangerous place for small creatures." The mantis tucked his front legs close to his chest, then pushed himself up with his little stick-shaped back legs, and his wings fanned out and beat him away into the shadows.

Kudzu had to admit something to himself that he didn't like: since he sometimes ate earthworms and grub worms, he must have seemed heartless and memoryless and guiltless, too. He hadn't understood that fact until this very moment. He didn't like the image of himself dining on another animal and looking like the praying mantis. No, he'd only eat plants, only nuts and fruits, from now on. He'd leave the predatory life to other predators. And if it was possible, if he found his way home, Kudzu would be content eating only kudzu for the rest of his life.

Kudzu's cheek pouches no longer made him feel special. Night was almost upon him, so Kudzu did not begin journeying for the kudzu patch or for anywhere else. Even if the patch beyond the maples was the one in his memories, he wouldn't reach it before the owls, raccoons, coyotes, and foxes began to wake and prowl the night. His pouches would serve no protection. So Kudzu did what he thought was best. Beneath a rock, he dug a hole just large enough for him to crawl into.

For hours, as he listened to the movement of larger creatures around him, he nervously stroked his tail, until finally, tired from shaking, he fell asleep.

CHAPTER 5

Quincy

Kudzu woke to the sound of streaming water. At least that was what he thought he'd heard. But when he climbed out of his hole beneath the rock, the woods were silent of the sound. Perhaps the wind's constant *shhhhhhushing* through the treetops had convinced the stream to hush. Or, perhaps, because of his thirst, he'd dreamed of water. But he didn't remember dreaming of water or of anything. He was living his dreams now. He was in the woods finally, wasn't he? Yet he didn't feel fulfilled. He still lacked something. He lacked water, but he also lacked something besides water. Something he couldn't name. Something he couldn't see or taste or hear, but it was something, all right. He felt the space in his gut where that something belonged, and he wanted it.

Kudzu began his first morning, perhaps his last morning, in the woods by aiming himself for the kudzu patch that lay someplace beyond the twin maples. He'd gone only a few steps when he heard the sound again. It was the delightful sound of movement, of freshness, of life. Yes, he was sure of it. He followed the sound through thorny underbrush and tree saplings. The sound would stop and start again, but Kudzu stayed on course, and he could hear that he was almost there. He was so close to water that his mouth watered. The streaming sound was coming from a small clearing just ahead of him, which smelled of pine—the smell of his dreams!

Kudzu parted the leaves of the last sapling that blocked his vision of the clearing, and he found himself almost face-to-face with the creator of the sound. Too scared to jump or run away or even to shriek, Kudzu stood where he was, frozen in the position of walking. Instead of a stream trickling through the clearing, there was a bed of needles below a pine tree, and on top of those needles, lying on top of that bed, was the black German shepherd, Kudzu's mortal enemy, licking an open wound.

What Kudzu had been hearing all this time was the sound of the dog tending to the gash across his ribs, where Mr. Weatherby had struck him with his hoe. The dog was so focused on his injury that he wasn't even aware of Kudzu's presence.

The longer Kudzu stood observing the dog nursing his wound and cleaning the blood from his fur, the more Kudzu viewed the shepherd not as a vicious alien with monstrous strength, but as an enormous chipmunk, like Owen himself, who could have been Kudzu's friend if life were different. The dog may not have freed Kudzu on purpose, but Kudzu was alive and free because of him, and the dog had been injured in the process.

Kudzu had to ask. He could not back away. Instinct took over as he took a single step forward into the clearing. "Are you okay?"

The shepherd turned away from his wound with ears pointing rigidly to the treetops. "Me?" he asked. Then he stretched his neck toward Kudzu so that his face and eyes and teeth were closer to Kudzu—and bigger, much bigger. "Why?" he growled.

"Well, I, I, I saw your wound there," Kudzu stuttered. "Are you all right?"

The dog's ears lay back down against his head. "What, this little cut?" he said. "I've had bigger flea bites than this. Don't you worry about me."

"It looks bad," said Kudzu.

"No, are you kidding?" The shepherd looked at his wound, as if for the first time, and gave it a gentle lick with his tongue.

"Sap from that pine tree would help seal it and let it heal," Kudzu told him.

The shepherd tilted his head up at the tree he'd been lying beneath. "So that's a pine tree, huh?"

"I'm sorry you got hurt," said Kudzu.

The shepherd turned back to Kudzu. "What did that man come after me for anyway? I didn't do anything to him."

"But you've been digging up his wife's flowers," said Kudzu.

"They belonged to somebody?" the shepherd asked. "Are you serious? Somebody can own flowers all to themselves? Is that legal?"

"I'm afraid it is," said Kudzu.

The dog's expression of disbelief relaxed, and he released a long, deep breath. "So," said the shepherd, "what did *you* do?"

"What did *I* do?" Kudzu patted the white of his chest. "*Me*?" He shook his head. "I didn't do anything."

"Then you're those people's pet?" the dog asked.

"No, of course not. I'm a chipmunk."

"Well, I can see you're a chipmunk. But you were in a cage for some reason."

"Because they trapped me in it!"

The shepherd crossed his front paws. "So, what did you do?"

"Nothing!"

"You had to do something."

"No," said Kudzu, "nothing at all. That's why it doesn't make sense."

"I know what you mean," said the shepherd. "I know what you mean."

Kudzu took a step closer and removed his acorn cap.

"Thank you for rescuing me."

The shepherd raised the whiskers of his eyebrows. "I rescued you?"

Kudzu nodded. "Mr. Weatherby was about to do me in with his hoe when you came along."

"He was?" The shepherd looked confused. "Then I got the hoe instead of you? That's...that's not fair."

"You saved my life," said Kudzu.

"How about that!" the shepherd laughed. "And I only wanted to play with it."

"You mean, you never meant to eat me?" asked Kudzu.

"Well," said the dog, "I wanted to do that, too. But after we played. I'm sorry."

Kudzu put his protective headgear back on.

"If it makes you feel any better," said the shepherd, "I'd rather eat a squirrel."

"How about eating plain, old dog food for a change?"

"Dog food doesn't grow on trees, you know," the shepherd said.

Kudzu opened his arms as if to say he wanted a hug, but what he wanted was the truth, whether painful or not. "Don't you have somebody to feed you?" he asked.

"Me," the shepherd said.

"You're all alone?"

The shepherd nodded his head.

"Is that legal?" asked Kudzu.

"No," the dog said, "it's not. If the dog catcher catches me, he'll kill me. That's why I'm hiding in these woods."

Kudzu stepped closer to this dog that saddened him. "You mean, you've never ever had a home?" he asked.

"Oh, no," the shepherd told him. "I've had a home before, but I don't want to go back to it. I don't want to be chained to a tree again. It's too easy to get tangled up and choke yourself when you're chained to a tree. And if you whine about it, you get kicked or something's thrown at you. And when it rains, that's even worse. But you better not say how you don't like it or how you're scared and cold because then you get kicked some more. No, I can live without a home like that."

Kudzu was reminded of something his parents had often told him—that there were more possibilities in this world than impossibilities, and that life could be as fruitful as your dreams. He was about to test if that was true. He shrugged his shoulders. "Maybe we can help each other," he said.

The dog smiled. "Maybe so."

Kudzu walked up to him and held out his paw. "I'm Kudzu."

The shepherd sniffed Kudzu's paw. "What do you have?"

Kudzu showed him that his paw was empty. "Nothing," he said. "I just want to shake."

The shepherd tilted his head. "Shake what?"

"Shake paws," said Kudzu.

"Why?" asked the shepherd.

"That's what animals do when they meet," Kudzu explained. "It's a sign of friendship. It's a promise that I won't eat you, if you won't eat me."

"Oh!" The dog raised his paw and grinned. "Nice to meet you, Kudzu," he said.

Kudzu took hold of a claw on one of the dog's toes and shook it. "And your name?" asked Kudzu.

The rare opportunity of sharing his name so excited the shepherd that his tongue fell out of his mouth. "I'm Quincy," he said proudly. "Quincy!"

"That is a good name," said Kudzu.

"Yeah!" said Quincy. "Isn't it? I heard someone read it off a street sign, and I decided to give it to myself."

"Your owner didn't give you one?"

Quincy shook his head. "Not a good one," he said. "That nasty man called me *Satan*. Who wants a name like that?"

"And your mother didn't give you one either?"

Quincy pressed his lips together and again shook his head.

"I never knew my mama," he said.

Kudzu tucked his tail underneath him, and he stroked it nervously. That's what he did whenever he felt lonely or sad, even for someone else.

After a moment, Kudzu said, "Quincy, how would you like to come with me and meet my mama?"

Quincy sat up, ready to go.

"First, though," said Kudzu, shaking a finger at him and giving Quincy his best I-mean-it look, "you've got to promise to be friendly and not eat her."

Quincy nodded obediently. "I promise."

"You can't eat *any* of my family," said Kudzu. "Not my daddy or anybody. Not even a houseguest."

"And they will all be *my* friends, too, right?" asked Quincy.

Kudzu smiled. "My friends are their friends," he said.

"Then I promise, Kudzu. I promise I won't eat another chipmunk as long as I live."

"And you won't need to, if you stick with me," Kudzu promised him. "There's plenty of food at my parents' house. They live under a thick patch of kudzu, and the vines are so tasty and so full of life they grow twelve of my feet in a day!" Kudzu stuck out one of his large hind feet.

Quincy flared his ears back. "Wow!" he said.

"And some of the most beautiful flowers you'll ever see bloom in that patch in late summer, like violets bunched together in the shape of a chipmunk's tail just to let the world know that God made it for us," Kudzu said, and he raised his tail high. "Just like my tail if you can imagine it purple."

Quincy smiled, but Kudzu frowned. He looked around, then raised his eyes to the sky. "If only I knew the way to go." Kudzu turned back to Quincy. "Would you happen to know where the kudzu patch is?"

"Which one?" Quincy asked.

Kudzu didn't know how to describe the location of his childhood home any better than how he had described it to the praying mantis the day before, so he said simply and honestly, "I don't know."

"Well," said Quincy, "I know where the nearest one is. It's right by a rusting pick-up truck with no tires, and inside on the floorboards, there is always rainwater that I can drink when I'm thirsty. Do you remember a pick-up being parked near your home?"

Kudzu's shoulders dropped in disappointment. He didn't remember anything but a circle of grass surrounding the patch. He shook his head.

"If you like, we could go there and at least get some water," said Quincy. "Then, we could go to another kudzu patch that I know about. Eventually, we're bound to find the right one."

Kudzu thought Quincy's plan was a good one. But they weren't ready to put it into action just yet. Kudzu told Quincy to lie back down, and Kudzu began scratching away a section of bark from the pine tree. When he'd uncovered a stream of sap, he gathered the thick, sticky syrup in his paws and spread it over Quincy's wound. The bleeding stopped immediately.

Quincy turned to his doctor and gave him a big lick on the face that lifted Kudzu off his feet and into the air. When Kudzu dropped back down, he held his paws up to stop Quincy from licking him again. "Okay, Quincy," he laughed. "You're welcome! You're welcome!"

But Quincy just smiled and licked him again. Kudzu kept laughing and telling Quincy to stay away and keep his tongue to himself, and Quincy kept licking him and licking him. When Quincy finally stopped, Kudzu looked like he'd been dunked in a river.

Together they then charged through the woods—Quincy leading the way and Kudzu scurrying to keep up. Kudzu never once looked above or behind him or to each side for dangerous predators hiding among the trees. Instead, Kudzu looked straight ahead, in the direction of his new friend, whose long tail waved about like a flag of fur. With Quincy, he now felt completely safe.

CHAPTER 6

The Kudzu Patch

Quincy led Kudzu out of the woods into a meadow of golden hay, an area of the farm Kudzu didn't remember ever seeing before. Here Mr. Weatherby had let the grass grow as tall as Quincy himself. And there must have been as many grasshoppers as there were falling stars. Every time Quincy would take a step forward, enough grasshoppers to feed an egret would hop out of his way. Then, as Quincy had promised, there appeared in the meadow an abandoned pick-up truck.

"Let me check it out first for snakes," said Quincy. He stood up on the passenger door, which had no window, and looked inside the truck.

"Well?" asked Kudzu.

"I don't see any snakes," said Quincy, "but you can't be too sure." He barked fiercely three times, and when nothing slithered or rattled, he told Kudzu that the coast was clear and the water was theirs. In a flash, Quincy had leaped over the door and was inside the truck lapping up water.

Kudzu had to find a different way to get inside. He walked around the truck first, then decided the best way was for him to jump onto the truck's front bumper. From there, he jumped onto the hood and scurried up the cracked windshield and onto the roof.

"Come to the door," he told Quincy, and when Quincy

stuck his head out the window, Kudzu dropped on top of his head and ran down Quincy's back to the truck seat. Kudzu was now only one small hop away from the floorboard's pool of rainwater. But when the smell of the sour water hit Kudzu's nose, he couldn't move any closer.

"It's not exactly Mrs. Weatherby's hose water, is it?" said Kudzu.

"I don't know," said Quincy. "Water's water, isn't it?"

Kudzu stared at the still, black water. He debated if he was even thirsty anymore.

"Go ahead," said Quincy. "It tastes pretty good. There's nothing wrong with it."

"Really? You think so?" asked Kudzu. The water looked so dark, anything could be in it, dead or alive. But he was so very thirsty. He hopped down onto the hill between the two floorboards. Maybe Quincy was right, Kudzu hoped. Maybe, he wondered, what felt wrong had nothing to do with the water and had everything to do with the direction their lives seemed to be heading.

"Go on," said Quincy.

Kudzu stretched out on his belly to drink the black, smelly water. "Well," he said, "here goes." Kudzu pinched his nose and touched the tip of his tongue to the water. He waited for the disgusting part to bite and make him sick, but when it didn't happen, Kudzu took a little sip.

"Well?" asked Quincy.

"Huh! You're right, it does taste pretty good," Kudzu said, with his nose still pinched, and his goose-like voice made Quincy laugh. Kudzu liked making Quincy laugh, so he kept his nose pinched and told Quincy to stop laughing, and that made Quincy laugh even harder. Pretending to be irritated by Quincy's wonderfully loud chuckling, Kudzu returned to the water and enjoyed its cool wetness as it went down his throat and filled his stomach.

Kudzu wiped his chin, then hopped back onto the seat

beside Quincy, who was pointing his paw directly ahead of them.

"The kudzu patch is not far from here," said Quincy. "Not far at all. Not at all."

Kudzu gazed through the truck's cracked windshield, as if through crisscrossing kudzu vines themselves, and imagined the exciting homecoming he was about to receive. His mother and father had never expected to see their children again. On the first day of spring, his parents had woken them from hibernation to begin digging out from their burrow. In the delightfully bright sunlight, his father announced to Kudzu and to each of Kudzu's brothers and sisters, "You have a life that you must live. It's time for you to go live it." His mother and then his father hugged each one of them. "Live it well," his mother said, sounding determined not to cry. "Live it right," his father said, sounding determined not to cry. And as all the children began to go their separate ways from home, Kudzu's father shouted, his voice cracking, "And live it long, dear ones!"

Kudzu smiled. He'd be the first chipmunk in history to return home. He looked up at Quincy, and Quincy smiled and his tail thumped against the seat.

"Let's go," said Kudzu.

"Then hop on," said Quincy.

Kudzu hopped on Quincy's back and started to crawl up to Quincy's head so that he could leave the way he entered, but Quincy surprised him with other plans.

"Hold on!" yelled Quincy, and suddenly Quincy sprang through the window. Kudzu's legs flew out from under him, but he was able to grab onto the long hair of Quincy's fur in time as Quincy flew through the air.

Kudzu squealed with delight. "Weeeeeeee!" he said, as they sailed like a bird above the tall grass, and as they dove like a bird into the tall grass. But it was like a shepherd that Quincy landed, on long legs cushioning the fall. Then Quincy's legs sprung them forward as he galloped like a horse in the direction Quincy had pointed in earlier.

Wouldn't his parents be amazed, thought Kudzu, when they see their son riding up on a dog?

As Quincy had promised, the meadow soon ended, and they found themselves at the edge of a kudzu patch. But this was a small patch, one much too small to be the right one. Kudzu wondered if this could even be called a patch. It was closer to being a garden, a well-defined kudzu garden boxed in between a meadow and a strip of bulldozed earth. The patch that had given Kudzu his name had covered twice as much ground as this one. But there did seem to be something familiar about this place. Maybe he was closer to home than he realized.

"Is this not it?" asked Quincy.

When Kudzu didn't answer, Quincy turned around and saw Kudzu lost in thought. Kudzu was carefully studying the slope of the land that lay before them in colorful stripes—first, the green kudzu, followed by the reddish-brown earth, which ran alongside the freshly tarred blacktop road.

"If you go down that road about two hours that way," said Quincy, pointing his nose to his left, where the road grew crooked, "you'll come to Quincy Boulevard. I don't know what this road's called, but Quincy Boulevard is that way, about two hours, I'd say."

Kudzu looked at Quincy. "We're not far from my home," he said. "This road, there's something about this road, about the way it bends. It's blacker than I remember." Then Kudzu shook his head. "But I'm not even sure I'm remembering it. I might only be imagining I've seen it."

The sound of an approaching car caught Kudzu's attention. He watched it pass by as it made a whooshing sound before it entered the bend of the road and disappeared behind a stand of trees. A wave of warmth suddenly washed over Kudzu, and he heard his mother speaking to him, as if she were standing before him now. "Stay away from the road," he recalled her saying. "Never go near it, and never cross it. Never, Kudzu. Never!"

He remembered all of it now. He remembered the road and the whooshing sound of cars, and he remembered promising his mother that he'd stay far away. And in order for him to keep his promise, he remembered how he'd decided to forget that the road and that side of the world ever existed, which was the reason he'd traveled the other way, toward Mrs. Weatherby's flowers, in the first place. But he didn't remember the space between the kudzu patch and the blacktop road. That was what confused him.

Kudzu hopped to the ground. "Wait here," he told Quincy, and he began searching through the kudzu vines for his old burrow. He found a couple of burrows owned by other chipmunks but none that struck his heart and made his body fill with warmth. He could feel he was close to home, yet he could also feel that he was far away from it, too. Finally, he decided to ask for directions.

Kudzu stuck his head down one of the chipmunk holes. "Hello!" he shouted. "Is anybody home?"

"Coming," he heard someone say in a deep but weak and shaking voice.

Kudzu pulled his head out of the hole and stepped back to wait. After a moment, a gray-haired chipmunk appeared with a tail thinning from age, perhaps the same age as Kudzu's father. But this was not Kudzu's father. This was no one Kudzu had ever met, or his nose would have told him so.

"How can I help you?" the old chipmunk asked.

Once Kudzu had explained to him what he was looking for and whom he was looking for, tears drained into the old chipmunk's eyes.

"That land over there you see cleared"—the old chipmunk pointed to the stretch of earth that was not kudzu and was not road—"that's where your home used to be."

Kudzu turned away and gazed through his own tears at the tire tracks in the earth.

"It was about a month ago," said the old chipmunk, "when people came with bulldozers to widen the road. We all thought if we stayed down in our homes, we'd be safe. Aren't we usually?"

Kudzu looked at him, and the old chipmunk shook his head. "I'm sorry, son," he said. "Those of us living here, just far enough away from the road, were lucky to survive, but down there, no one was lucky. Not where the bulldozing took place. No one."

Anger rose in Kudzu so strong and quick that he felt he was actually growing. "The Weatherbys did this?" he asked.

"Who?" said the old chipmunk.

"The people who own this land," explained Kudzu.

"Oh, then no," said the old chipmunk. "It wasn't them. The way I heard it told was that the county government forced them to give up that strip of land so the road could be widened for progress. That's what I heard anyway."

Kudzu realized that by having no one specific he could be angry at, he couldn't stay angry. He was now beginning to lose all emotion and instead feel completely empty and lost.

The old chipmunk stroked his beard. "I've never seen progress before, but it must be awfully big to need more than two lanes of road. Maybe too big, don't you think?" The old chipmunk patted his plump belly. "Not that I shouldn't watch my diet and exercise more myself."

Kudzu turned to look behind him at the ground that sloped upward toward the meadow, and Kudzu's emptiness suddenly filled with fear. He didn't see Quincy where he was supposed to be. He didn't see him anywhere.

"Quincy!" called Kudzu. He called again, as loud as he could, and Quincy popped up out of the leafy vines with a sleepy grin on his face.

Seeing his loyal friend, the only friend he had in the whole world, made Kudzu want to forget where he was and put the kudzu patch behind him forever. Without another word to the old chipmunk, Kudzu instantly began to run.

Quincy waited where he was told, but he grew bigger and bigger and his barks became louder and louder as Kudzu

gradually felt warmer and warmer, until Kudzu was there with Quincy. Holding one of Quincy's legs, Kudzu started to cry, and he didn't stop for a long, long time.

CHAPTER 7

With a Bird's Eyes

Quincy had no magic words of wisdom to soothe his little friend. He'd learned from his own life of sad times that there weren't any such words. He instead showed his wisdom by gently picking Kudzu up in his mouth and setting his friend on his back and carrying him away, through the tall grass of the meadow, to a place with better memories.

When Quincy had reached the clearing in the woods where Kudzu and Quincy had first met, Quincy lowered Kudzu down onto the bed of pine needles and curled himself around Kudzu to let him know he was not alone and was protected. Maybe only time would heal Kudzu's wounded heart, but sleep, thought Quincy, would make time speed more quickly by.

They had been asleep for hours when Kudzu woke fast from his dreams and looked up at the pine tree soaring tall above them, seeming to reach so high in the sky that its needles must have tickled the moon. He'd forgotten all about the pine in his dreams until just now, having dreamed about it, and he wondered if this tree, the one right here, was the same one he'd gazed at so many times from the flowerbed. Was this the one that stood taller than all the other trees and reappeared in his dreams? If he were to climb it, what would he see?

Careful not to wake Quincy, Kudzu eased himself up and

tiptoed away from the smile-shaped curve of Quincy's body. Then, just as carefully, Kudzu latched his claws around the bark of the trunk, and he began to climb. But very slowly and very quietly. And the climbing upward seemed to take forever. The tree kept going up and going up, just like in his dreams, but as long as he climbed, he never tired. He seemed instead to gather strength. Maybe this tree, he thought, would lead him to heaven and he would see his mom and dad again. Maybe there was power in dreaming after all.

The trunk gradually narrowed and eventually split into three branches. Kudzu took the one growing upward rather than outward, and at the end of that branch, he found himself in the sky itself, with nothing above him except the moon. This was not heaven, but there was something heavenly about this angle of vision, which quickly put his past below, the past of his entire life, in the proper perspective. From here, the Weatherbys' house looked small and ridiculous to him now, and the flowerbed beside it even more so. And the slope of the hill he had tumbled down with the help of Quincy, it seemed no deeper than a human footprint, and the pecan trees were no bigger than his paws.

Kudzu shifted around the branch, and to the north he saw what he knew was the dusty, bulldozed earth where his childhood home had been. But from atop the pine tree that strip of land could have been a bread crust that Mrs. Weatherby had tossed out for the birds. And the road, blacker than the night sky, was no wider than the stripes down his back. Maybe this was how you were supposed to look at items of your past. You don't forget them, but you view them with a bird's eyes so that what you see large as life is only what you *have* and not what you *had* or think you *should have had*, so that you never take what is in front of you and who is beside you for granted. Maybe that was the lesson his parents had been trying to teach their children. Maybe that was why his parents had never expected to see their children again. His parents understood that they wouldn't live forever and that their children needed to learn to take care of themselves.

Kudzu smiled with pride, thinking of his wise parents. He turned his head westward and was looking for nothing in particular, but it was then when he found it. The subject of many of his father's bedtime stories. What his father had claimed to have seen himself once, and had touched once, and had even drunk from once. There in the horizon, exactly as Kudzu had dreamed, flowed the Mississippi River. And like a bending road after a heavy shower, it sparkled with silver moonlight. This was proof, thought Kudzu. Dreams do come true.

Something occurred to him then, and he turned northward and looked at the blacktop road of his youth, then again at the river of now. He was amazed by their likeness, how they each curled through the land like snakes in motion, or like...yes, he thought, like sleeping dogs! All along without knowing it, while he'd been sleeping, he'd been dreaming of home. Not the home of used to be, with his parents, and not the home of what he had, in the flowerbed, but the one that would be, that he would have someday, with Quincy. Maybe right here in the woods at the base of this very wonderful tree.

In that instant, his mind played a trick on him. He heard what sounded like a car whooshing by. But how could that be, so far above the road, up here in a tree? He shook his head. It made no sense for him to look behind him in case a car was actually coming, but he turned to look anyway—and when he did, he saw a barn owl soaring toward him, its white face just inches away, and its talons stretched open to snatch him up.

Kudzu did the quickest thing he could think of to escape the owl: he let go of the branch. And as he was falling backward, he watched the owl's talons close around the empty branch and snap it in two.

Seeing how near death he'd come, Kudzu began to scream. But as he continued to fall backward, he began to scream from a different fear—that he'd never stop falling. That's when the owl swooped around and came flying after him, so Kudzu started screaming from that. He was falling and he was screaming, and the owl was gaining on him. Suddenly, a branch caught Kudzu's fall, and he landed with a *whumpf*. He scrambled to clutch onto the branch with the claws of his hind feet and then sprang away for the tree trunk, barely missing again the owl's strike. But the chase wasn't over.

Kudzu scurried down the trunk, zig-zagging through the branches, while the owl circled and attacked, circled and attacked.

"Quincy!" hollered Kudzu, running for his life. "Quincy! Quincy!"

Quincy had been awake since Kudzu's long and frightful scream, but Quincy had mistaken that for a hungry baby bird throwing a temper tantrum, so he'd closed his eyes and was trying to go back to sleep. But now, hearing his name called out, Quincy realized that Kudzu had to be in the pine high above. He jumped to his paws and looked up into the tree, but couldn't see his chipmunk friend anywhere.

"Kudzu!" Quincy shouted. "Where are you? What's wrong?" Then he saw the owl attacking, circling and attacking. Quincy leaped against the tree trunk. "Leave him alone!" he barked. He tried climbing the tree to go after the owl himself, but his claws failed to hold up his weight, and he fell right back down.

"Quincy!" Kudzu continued to shout while dodging limbs and talons, and he repeated his call again and again so that Quincy would always know how far away he was. Without knowing it, Quincy was doing the same for Kudzu. By growling and barking threats at the owl, Kudzu always knew how far away Quincy was, which helped Kudzu to judge the distance between himself and safety. Kudzu knew if he did ever stop and take his eyes off of what lay directly in front of him to look for Quincy that would be when the owl would catch him.

The branches started to thin out, providing him much less protection against the owl's attacks, so Kudzu borrowed one of the owl's own strategies. He began circling the tree, as though he were going down a spiral staircase. The owl, however, could circle faster on its wings than Kudzu could on his feet. The owl was catching up with him, and the owl was laughing about it.

Quincy began to sound closer, too—so close and loud it was as if Kudzu and Quincy were crammed together in a burrow and Quincy, for a Quincy reason, had suddenly decided to shout in his ear. That was when Kudzu stopped running. When Kudzu flung himself away from the tree and flew into the air, as though he too were an owl. And when Quincy saw him soaring and saw the owl soaring behind him even faster, he too flung himself into the air and stretched open his mouth.

Perhaps it seemed odd to the owl that a chipmunk would escape its outstretched talons by flying right into the fangs of a dog. But it must have seemed stranger when the dog set the chipmunk safely on the ground and defended him.

"Get out of here!" Quincy shouted. But he was actually hoping the owl would come closer. Quincy had eaten only grass and dirt for the last three days, so he guessed an owl could be quite tasty.

The owl perched himself on the nearest limb out of reach and sneered at Quincy. "You ought to mind your own business, you interloper!" the owl told him.

"Yeah, the day you start picking on somebody your own size," snapped Quincy. "You barn chicken!"

"You ignorant, domesticated carnivore," said the owl.

"You flat-faced redneck pigeon," answered Quincy. He was starting to drool.

Disgusted, the owl turned away, his head smoothly rotating in the opposite direction, then his body twisted underneath him, and he flew off.

"Thanks," said Kudzu, sprawled out on his back and panting, with his acorn cap sitting crooked on his head.

"Of course, anytime, Kud." Quincy eased himself down beside Kudzu on the pine needles. "So," he said, "what were you doing up there? Looking for food? I know I could use some."

Kudzu didn't feel like talking about what he *had* been doing. He wanted to talk about what he was *going* to do. And what he was going to do, said Kudzu, was find a way to live again on the Weatherbys' farm, where there was food enough and room enough and pure beauty enough for everyone. "This is no place for a chipmunk or a dog," he explained, and Quincy's ears stood straight up, like Native American arrowheads, which his old owner would hunt for and sometimes find along the banks of a nearby creek or swimming hole.

"You've stopped digging up the flowers, so I think you're okay now," said Kudzu, "but we've got to find out why the Weatherbys came after me. If we can find that out, then I'll stop doing whatever it is they don't like. Then, I'll be okay, too."

"But how will we ever learn the reason why?" asked Quincy.

"There's only one way," said Kudzu. He sat up on his knees. "We've got to go to the source. We've got to go to the Weatherbys themselves. That's how." He pushed himself to his feet, and his legs wobbled. "But you'll have to carry me there, if you don't mind. I'm pooped!"

"Mind?" said Quincy. "Look, I've had ticks ride my back that were bigger than you. Anytime you want a lift, just hop on."

"Well," said Kudzu, "all right." He climbed up and patted Quincy on the head. "I'm ready whenever you are," he said, but Quincy wasn't ready yet. Quincy wanted to be patted on the head a while longer. And once Kudzu had patted him on the head a while longer, Quincy stood up and happily trotted toward the Weatherbys' farmhouse.

CHAPTER 8

Stanley

On the way to the farmhouse that early morning, before the sun had risen and while the rooster slept, Kudzu and Quincy stopped at the pecan orchard to fill their bellies. Kudzu suggested that they first gather the pecans into a pile, then shell and split them together. Quincy had never practiced that much self-control, that much planning. He'd always eaten as much as he could right then and there. He'd never once planned for the future, which was what chipmunks did all the time.

"I'll give it a try," said Quincy, and he meant well, but as soon as he put his teeth around the hard, bone-like shell of the first pecan, he chomped into it. Though once he'd chewed it into a gritty, bitter casserole, he couldn't bring himself to swallow. He made a yuck face at Kudzu instead and spat it out. "That's about as bad as eating a moth!" said Quincy. "I'll stick to grass and dirt from now on."

"No," laughed Kudzu, "you just didn't do it right. Let me show you." Kudzu gnawed at a pecan until he'd cracked it open. Then, with his tiny claws and his long, front teeth, he pulled one of the halves clean from the shell. "Try it this way," he said, holding the golden meat out for Quincy, but Quincy was slow to take it. He wanted to smell it first.

"This is the last chance I'm giving these things," Quincy said.

"And that's all it will take," said Kudzu.

Quincy took the pecan half into his mouth and chewed it once, then stopped. "Hey," he said, "this one's soft. Tastes pretty good." Rather than chewing the pecan half any further, he swallowed it so that he could hurry and have some more. But there was no such thing as eating pecans in a hurry. To eat them required a lot of work. And to feed a dog the size of Quincy, that practically required a lifelong career in pecan shelling.

Kudzu filled his belly on three pecans, but Quincy was still hungry after eating twenty of them. Not only was Kudzu too tired to shell any more, but they had also run out of time. The sun was rising now. The rooster was crowing. And that meant the Weatherbys would be starting their day soon, too, and might see them. So Kudzu hopped on Quincy's back and rode him to the house. Kudzu knew of a special entryway underneath the kitchen.

The Weatherbys' house was not the typical farmhouse. Unlike most others, which were built of pressed wood shavings from the hardware store, this one was made solid from the trees that had once stood on the very land where it was sitting. When Mr. Weatherby was a young man, he had chopped down a cluster of giant cedar trees himself, and on top of the tree stumps, he began building a house that would be a lasting home for him and his new wife.

The Weatherbys' house was now forty years old, but the boards were still in good condition and were always given a fresh coat of white paint every three years. Nevertheless, anything will grow tired and shift over time. Things change as they settle down. So over the years, as the boards relaxed, a space here and there had opened up between them. Kudzu remembered seeing a mouse who would go in and out of the house through one of those spaces.

When Kudzu and Quincy had reached the house, Kudzu climbed down from Quincy and walked underneath it. Quincy followed, crawling on his belly.

"Hey," whispered Quincy, "why don't we live under here?" It was dark below the floor of the house, and the dusty ground was pleasantly cool to his belly. "We would be safe from the rain, and the Weatherbys would never find us here."

Kudzu turned around, then stood up on his toes and stretched out his arms. "Quincy, I could live here, easily," he said. "But would you be happy never to walk or run again for the rest of your life?"

"Good point," said Quincy.

Kudzu continued forward, to the cedar stump that was below the Weatherbys' kitchen. But before climbing up and entering the space between the boards, he spoke to Quincy once more. "Don't make a sound," Kudzu whispered.

Quincy shook his head. "I won't," he said.

"Shhhhh," said Kudzu.

Quincy nodded. "Shhhhh," he promised.

Kudzu then crawled up the stump and squeezed himself through the hole. He found himself in a long, narrow room filled with an enormous assortment of human goods. There were buttons of different colors and sizes neatly stacked, and there were paper clips and pennies and rubber bands. And between postage stamps decorating the walls, there were more and more items piled on shelves. Kudzu passed through a maze of bobby pins, needles, and spools of thread, past nails, Band-Aids, and Christmas-tree lights. And somewhere up ahead there was food. Kudzu could smell it. But before he found what must have been dried meat of some rare kind, he stumbled upon the owner of this room, the mouse himself, sitting up on a nest of cotton balls and reading a matchbook cover.

"Yes?" the mouse asked. He laid his matchbook cover down on his lap and was looking at Kudzu through a pair of glasses. "May I help you?"

"Uh...." Kudzu forgot for a moment why he'd come. "Sorry, excuse me," Kudzu said. "I've never seen a mouse wearing a pair of glasses before."

"And I assure you," said the mouse, "nor have I ever seen a chipmunk wearing a cap."

Kudzu smiled, and the mouse stepped away from his nest to greet Kudzu with a pawshake.

"I'm Stanley," said the mouse. "Nice to finally meet you, Kudzu."

Kudzu's body went limp, and he stopped shaking Stanley's paw. "How do you know my name?"

"Are you kidding? You're one of the favorite subjects of discussion in this household." Stanley's glasses slid down his nose, and he pushed them back up. "I try to know everything that is going on around here. Knowledge," he said, pointing at his own head, "is what keeps this little rodent alive–and living well, I might add."

Kudzu leaned forward to examine Stanley's pair of wire-rim glasses. "Where did you find those?"

Stanley removed them and held them up for the taller Kudzu to see. "I didn't find them," he said. "I found the parts, but I made the glasses myself. The frame is a twist-tie from a bag of bread, and the lenses are contacts that the Weatherbys' daughter once lost while visiting." Stanley put his glasses back on. "That's why I collect so much of what the Weatherbys have lost or thrown away. There's no way of knowing what I'll need to make for myself tomorrow."

"Tomorrow," nodded Kudzu. "I understand." He was thinking of winter, how he had lost his storage room of nuts when he had lost his burrow. He was no longer prepared for tomorrow, and it concerned him.

"So tell me, Kudzu," said Stanley, "why have you come here today?"

Kudzu nervously stroked his tail. He explained how he'd tried to live elsewhere, but the farm appeared to be the only place left for him to live. "I've come to you," said Kudzu, "hoping to learn why the Weatherbys don't like me anymore. Why they trapped me and wanted to kill me. I need to know what I did to deserve death, so I can stop doing whatever that is and do something different and get to live below the flowers again and be safe again. The way life used to be."

Stanley held his paws together. "Well, Kudzu, I'm afraid," he said, with big, black apologetic eyes, "that's not going to be possible. You can never live below the flowers again, I'm afraid. Maybe somewhere else on the farm but not in the flowerbed—*ever*. They are prepared now to do anything to keep you out of there. *Anything*."

Kudzu sat down on the edge of Stanley's nest of cotton. He looked at his knees and rubbed them. "But why?" he asked. "I never did anything to hurt the flowers. Those were my flowers, too. It was Quincy, the shepherd dog. He didn't mean to. He didn't know what he was doing. But it was him who made a mess of the flowers. Not me."

"And why do you think he did that?" asked Stanley.

"Well, to dig me up, of course," said Kudzu.

"And that's why you can't live there."

"But that's not right," said Kudzu. "He's responsible for his own behavior, just like everybody else, isn't he?"

Stanley shrugged. "Sometimes."

"If the Weatherbys wanted to get rid of a dog," asked Kudzu, "then why wouldn't they just put out a dog trap? Isn't that the logical thing to do?"

Stanley shook his head. "People don't make dog traps. They make rodent traps—for squirrels and rats, and for you and me."

Kudzu started to grow angry at the injustice, but then he thought of Quincy's kind and loyal nature and was glad there weren't dog traps. He took a deep breath, and as he released it slowly, he did more than accept the world as it was. He realized that he was more responsible for the way of the world than he had ever imagined. If he hadn't been so greedy and lazy and spoiled to insist upon living in luxury that even his parents in the kudzu patch did not experience, none of Mrs. Weatherby's flowers would've been destroyed, and Quincy wouldn't have been injured with a hoe. Maybe the Weatherbys would've even taken Quincy in as a pet and kept him fed. And if Kudzu had first chosen to live in the pecan orchard or in the back pasture near the vegetable garden or in the side yard by the chicken coop, he would still have a home and would be prepared for winter. But, then again, if Kudzu had lived life differently, he and Quincy might not have become friends, so Kudzu stopped dreaming of things he should've done and began thinking of what he should do, and where he and Quincy should live.

Kudzu turned to Stanley. "I can learn to work a little harder and dig where the weeds are, can't I?" he asked, and Stanley nodded. "I can learn to live without the convenience of hose water. I can walk a little farther for a drink, can't I?" he asked, and Stanley nodded his head. "And I can always see the flowers from a distance and visit them on occasion, can't I?" asked Kudzu.

Stanley smiled. "I don't believe the Weatherbys would mind that at all. In fact," he said, turning up his ears, "here they come now." The floor began to vibrate, and Kudzu was looking around him on all sides, trying to figure out which way the Weatherbys were coming from.

"Follow me," Stanley told him, and he led Kudzu through the rest of the maze. They passed piles of meat pellets in curious shapes and cooking spices that were separated into caps from toothpaste tubes. Then they came to an opening in the wall, and Stanley stepped through it, into brighter light.

When Kudzu came to the opening himself, he saw it was safe to walk out into the room because there was an enormous fence up ahead that guarded the mouse hole. It looked to Kudzu like a fence, so that was what he thought it was. But it was actually a screen below a refrigerator. Stanley walked up to the holes in the screen, which offered a clear view of one of the rooms in the house. Kudzu hurried to catch up.

Kudzu was shocked by what he saw. Mr. Weatherby took a pot of mud from a machine and poured some of the mud into a cup. He sat down on a stool and blew on the cup of mud. Steam rose, and then he poured some of the mud from the cup into a saucer. Carefully, he raised the saucer to his mouth and blew on the steaming mud twice more before doing what Kudzu had never thought a human would do. Mr. Weatherby sipped that mud! Not only that, he drank that saucer dry and then filled it up again! Not until that very moment had Kudzu considered how similar humans were to mosquitoes.

Kudzu looked at Stanley, who couldn't seem to believe his eyes either.

"Does he do this every morning?" Kudzu asked.

Stanley nodded. "Every morning," he said. "And why he prefers that to sweet tea, I'll never understand." He pointed at Mrs. Weatherby standing at the stove, then began stroking his whiskers as he stared in her direction with dreamy eyes. "But what Mrs. Weatherby cooks for breakfast," Stanley told Kudzu, "that I'll always understand and will never forget. Oh, Kudzu," he said, licking his lips and stroking his whiskers faster than before, "it's simple and basic, extremely high in cholesterol and very fattening, but the taste and texture both are most refined."

"Exquisite?" asked Kudzu.

Stanley smiled as though he was impressed with the accuracy of Kudzu's educated vocabulary. "Indeed," he said. "Exquisite, indeed."

"I sure hope that fox," said Mr. Weatherby, "didn't find another way into the chicken coop last night."

Mrs. Weatherby continued to stir the contents of one of the pots. "I know," she muttered quietly, without looking at her husband, as if she were simply speaking aloud to herself. As if she were praying. "I know," she said.

"If we lose any more," said Mr. Weatherby, "we might as well stop raising chickens."

Mrs. Weatherby removed the spoon from the pot, covered the pot, and glanced away, in the direction of the window.

Kudzu tugged on Stanley's arm. "She's looking at the flowers," he said in a hushed but excited voice. He had never imagined a morning when he would be on this side of the window.

"She does that every morning," Stanley told him.

"I know," said Kudzu dreamily. "I know."

"You were able to out-fox that dog," said Mrs. Weatherby. She turned away from the window and smiled at her husband. "You'll do the same with that fox."

"But when?" said Mr. Weatherby.

Mrs. Weatherby removed the lid from a cast-iron skillet, and a cloud of steam rose up. "You better wake Owen," she said. "This is almost ready."

Mr. Weatherby nodded as he raised the saucer to his lips and sipped once more what Kudzu would forever believe was a beverage of mud. "That boy is so smart, you can tell." He set his saucer on the counter behind him and stood from his stool. "But when will he speak? Do you think he even can?"

Mrs. Weatherby shook her head. “I never imagined those ear infections as a baby would lead to this. We just gotta pray and keep working with him.”

“Most three-year-olds are singing the alphabet by now, aren’t they?” he asked.

Mrs. Weatherby nodded. “He will, too.”

“But when?” asked Mr. Weatherby. “I worry how much he’s falling behind. I sure thought his surgery would have helped more by now. It’s not like he’s hearing under water anymore, right? The tubes they put in his ears let him hear good as new, right?”

Mrs. Weatherby nodded. She stirred what was in the skillet and nodded again. “Progress will come, honey. Now, you better go wake Owen. Breakfast is ready.”

CHAPTER 9

A Sliver of Moon, a Roof, and a Telephone Pole

Stanley explained to Kudzu what the Weatherbys were talking about when they had mentioned Owen's surgery and the tubes implanted in his ears. What Mr. Weatherby had said about Owen having heard the world as if he were underwater now made sense to him because that must have been like how he heard things from underground. Those tubes were escape tunnels! That was the only way Kudzu could wrap his head around the notion that tubes existed inside Owen's head. Now Owen wasn't trapped anymore inside a cage of silence and confusion. He was free. Well, he was free to hear. If only adult humans would learn to slow down and listen more to the many languages of the smaller creatures, Owen could also be free to be heard.

Once the Weatherbys finished breakfast, Mr. Weatherby collected the dishes and began washing them, while Mrs. Weatherby read the news aloud from the morning paper and while Owen drew beside her in a coloring book. Seeing the Weatherbys share the duties of the household reminded Kudzu of how he grew up, with everyone helping one another around the burrow. Realizing that a human's heart was like that of a chipmunk's gave Kudzu an idea, and that idea quickly grew into a plan.

Excited about his new plan, Kudzu turned to Stanley and shook his paw. "Thanks for bringing me here," Kudzu told him. Then he explained that he had a friend waiting for him outside, and he wondered if Stanley could help his friend, who was very hungry and very big.

Stanley led Kudzu back into his home between the walls. He pointed at the pellets of meat that he had separated into piles according to their shapes. "He can have as many as he wants," Stanley said.

Kudzu picked up a pellet from the first pile and examined it. "What is it?" he asked. It was shaped like the letter C, but since Kudzu had never seen the letter C before, he wondered why the pellet was shaped like a sliver of the moon. Those of the second pile, which were shaped like A's, looked to Kudzu like the roofs of houses. And those of the third pile looked more like telephone poles than T's. The pellets may have had different shapes, but they all smelled the same—like something he had never eaten before.

"That's cat food. Liver flavored," Stanley said. "Does your friend like liver?"

Kudzu didn't know. "He likes meat. Liver is meat, right?"

"That's right," said Stanley. "Liver comes from a cow. It's a cow's liver."

"And you're sure I can have all of these?" asked Kudzu. There might have been a week's worth of food here for a mouse, but Kudzu believed his cheeks could hold every pellet.

"Just leave me three of them, just three, if you don't mind," said Stanley. "The Weatherbys always eat at the potluck dinner at church on church night, so there won't be any leftovers for me to find tomorrow night in the garbage can." He shook his head. "You wouldn't believe how much they throw away."

"Well, I appreciate this," said Kudzu, "and so will Quincy, I know." Kudzu wasted no time. He began packing the pellets into the pockets of his cheeks.

"So, who is Quincy?" Stanley asked. "Another chipmunk?"

Kudzu stopped working so that he could speak. "A dog," he said.

Stanley's eyes grew enormous behind the lenses of his glasses. "The one...?" he started to say, but he was too surprised to finish his question.

"The one who dug up the flowers, who chased me and wanted to eat me?" asked Kudzu. "Yes," he answered. "The very same one."

"Wow, can that be?" asked Stanley. "I've never heard of a chipmunk and a dog becoming friends." He scratched behind his ears. "I guess I need to get out more often."

Kudzu nodded with a smile. "I've learned the same lesson myself." He picked up another pellet, packed it into his mouth, and continued doing the same with others.

Stanley stood aside and silently watched Kudzu work for a moment, but then decided to join in and help Kudzu by handing him the pellets. By the time they had reached the end of each pile and there was only one C, one A, and one T left for Stanley to eat tomorrow night on church night, Kudzu's cheeks were bulging to nearly the size of Stanley himself.

"Well, that's it." Stanley pushed his glasses up to the bridge of his nose, then rested his paws on his hips. "It was nice meeting you, Kudzu. Come back any time."

Unable to speak, Kudzu waved goodbye and turned around very slowly and waddled out, being careful not to bump his cheeks into Stanley's neatly arranged goods. When he reached the hole between the boards, Kudzu had to exit one cheek at a time, before finally squeezing his body through.

"Kudzu!" shouted Quincy. "I was beginning to think I'd never see you again and I would have to live under the house by myself for the rest of my life. I wouldn't be able to walk again or run again, but I wouldn't want to, Kudzu. Not alone, not by myself. So I stayed here and waited for you, and I waited and waited. I would've waited forever!" He watched Kudzu crawl down the stump backward, facing the other direction. And when Kudzu reached the ground and turned and faced Quincy, Quincy's jaw dropped and his tongue fell out. "What on earth happened to your mouth? Did you get in a fight? Kudzu, did somebody hurt you?" Quincy growled. "Who did this to you?"

Kudzu couldn't explain anything to Quincy. All Kudzu could do was empty his mouth to show what he had brought for him. With his paws pressed against his cheeks, he began pushing the cat food out of the deep pockets of his cheeks. One by one the letters dropped out of his mouth.

Quincy was amazed—more amazed even than hungry. "How do you hold so much in there?" he asked, but Kudzu still couldn't answer him. Letters and the words they spelled kept coming.

When the last CAT had been pushed out of Kudzu's mouth, Kudzu smiled. "For you," he said.

"For me?" asked Quincy. He sniffed the pile of sticky letters, and his eyes widened.

"You don't mind that they're a little wet, do you?" asked Kudzu. "It's cat food from a cow's liver. Have you ever eaten cat food?"

"No," said Quincy, "but it smells pretty good." He tasted one of the A's, and it tasted as though an A were the grade it deserved. So Quincy served himself again, finishing off the pile of pellets in two gulps. "I could eat a lot more where that came from," Quincy said, licking his lips.

"That's all the mouse had to offer," Kudzu told him, "but, Quincy, something occurred to me while I was in the house. I think I may have a plan for us. A plan for everybody. And if it goes right, I think it could bring you all the food you would ever need."

Quincy's ears stood up and brushed the floor of the house.

Kudzu removed his cap and set it on the ground, and then

he sat on the crown of his cap so that he could have a little more height and meet Quincy eye to eye. "The Weatherbys are having a problem with a fox getting into their chicken coop and eating their chickens," he explained. "Since you and I caused them trouble before, I think it would be right for us to help them with this fox problem. What do you think, Quincy? Do you think you could catch a fox?"

"I don't know," said Quincy. "I've never seen a fox. How big is one?"

"Smaller than you, I believe," Kudzu said.

"Well, I guess," said Quincy. "I can give it a try."

"It wouldn't hurt you to become a hero," said Kudzu, but Kudzu could tell that Quincy hadn't completely understood what he had said. Quincy nodded, but his eyes still looked blank. "The Weatherbys would probably like to have a hero for a pet," Kudzu explained further. "And they would treat you like a hero and feed you every day," he said, and Quincy's eyes sparkled. "So do you think you could find the fox?"

"I don't know," said Quincy. "I don't have the nose of a hunting dog. That's what I need–a hunting dog's nose, like a hound dog's nose. I'm a shepherd, a working dog. My nose works, but it doesn't hunt."

"Protecting chickens is work," said Kudzu.

"But I've got to eat more than a few pieces of cat food if I'm going to have enough strength to chase and fight a fox," said Quincy. "Especially a fox that's been eating so well on chickens!"

Kudzu stood up, brushed the dirt from his cap, and put his cap back on his head. "Good point. But, Quincy," he said, "I have the answer." Kudzu hopped on Quincy's back and directed him to the persimmon trees, which grew near the chicken coop in the side yard.

When they arrived at the persimmon trees, Kudzu dropped to the ground and picked up one of the reddish-orange persimmons that had been ripe enough recently to fall from one of the limbs. He held it out for Quincy to take a bite, and when Quincy did, persimmon juice squirted all over Kudzu's face.

Quincy laughed—but then the flavor of the fruit hit his taste buds and he suddenly quit laughing and gagged. "Gross! Disgusting!" Quincy howled. He quickly ate a mouthful of grass to clean the persimmon taste off his tongue. "They taste like juicy pecans with the shells still on!"

"I happen to think they're delicious," said Kudzu, wiping his face with his paws and licking them.

Quincy turned his head away. "Let me know when you're done," he said. "I can't watch you do that." With his head turned the other way, he saw the rooster perched on his favorite fence post. Quincy walked up to him.

"Excuse me, Mr. Rooster," said Quincy, and the rooster stood up and stuck out his red chest. He was daring Quincy to come any closer to the chicken yard.

"Would you happen to know," asked Quincy, "where the fox lives?" What Quincy didn't understand was that neither a chicken nor a rooster was able to carry on a reasonable conversation about a fox. If they even heard the word *fox*, they went insane with fear. And that's what happened to the rooster. Suddenly, the rooster's proud, strong chest deflated like a popped balloon.

"Fox?! Fox?!" the rooster crowed, and when the chickens housed in the chicken coop heard the rooster's urgent warning, they too began crying and screeching and beating their wings together—trying to fly away but forgetting that they were unable to fly and simply bouncing into each other.

Kudzu tapped Quincy on the leg. "Please, don't do that again."

"Oh, don't you worry," said Quincy. "I don't believe I ever will."

Kudzu climbed up on Quincy's back. "I've got another idea," he said, then directed Quincy to the bird feeders, which hung from the oak tree between the flowerbed and the farmhouse. It was from this tree that Kudzu for so long had collected his acorns and his acorn caps.

The Weatherbys had nailed an aluminum skirt to the trunk of the oak tree to prevent squirrels from climbing up the tree and eating all the seeds in the bird feeders. Having a dog for a friend, however, encouraged Kudzu to become more creative than he'd ever dreamed possible. Kudzu told Quincy to stop underneath one of the feeders, then Kudzu held on as tightly as he could to Quincy's fur.

"Now, stand up," said Kudzu. So Quincy stood up on his hind legs, and when he did, the gold and purple finches scattered to the treetops. Kudzu then leaped from Quincy's neck to the feeder. Once he had a firm hold on the feeder, Kudzu told Quincy to open his mouth, and he began shoveling the little, round millet seeds out of the feeder. They rained down into Quincy's open mouth. "Well, what do you think?" Kudzu asked. He stopped shoveling and looked down. "How do they taste?"

Quincy chewed and chewed, but the seeds were so small that he had a hard time chewing them. Eventually, he gave up and swallowed, but even swallowing them was difficult. Many of them remained stuck to the sides of his mouth and to his gums and tongue.

Quincy coughed, and seeds flew from his mouth. "They're awfully dry!" he said, losing more seeds as he spoke.

"Just what do you think you are doing now?" a familiar voice asked Kudzu in a scolding manner.

Kudzu turned around and saw Victoria, the monarch butterfly, hanging beside him, her wings keeping her afloat.

"I'm trying to help this dog help the Weatherbys," Kudzu explained.

"You are the type who never learns anything," she told him. "You're a troublemaker. But worse, you are an ingrate, Kudzu. A vain and hopeless ingrate."

Quincy grew furious hearing this butterfly insult Kudzu with words only she could understand. So Quincy decided to insult her with nonsense she couldn't understand. Quincy barked and he barked. And he sprang into the air to bark more nonsense into her ears. But he was barking so loud that he and Kudzu didn't hear the Weatherbys open the door of the house and rush out onto the porch.

"Go on, you! Get away from there!" Mr. Weatherby shouted.

Quincy stopped barking and looked at the Weatherbys.

"Shoo! Shoo!" added Mrs. Weatherby, waving her arms.

Owen stepped up between his grandparents and chimed in with an eye-crossing scream that finally softened into laughter.

Quincy looked up at Kudzu for advice on what to do.

"Stay right where you are," said Kudzu.

"Ga!" Owen shrieked.

Quincy turned and saw the boy was pointing at him and chanting, "Ga, ga, ga!"

Kudzu dropped from the bird feeder onto Quincy's back, and Kudzu could tell by the Weatherbys' reaction of surprise that they hadn't noticed him hanging onto the feeder. They had seen only the dog leaping into the air and barking at a butterfly. But now they watched the dog running away, with a chipmunk clinging onto his back. Mr. and Mrs. Weatherby glanced at each other in amazement, while the boy between them yelled, "Ka-ga, ka-ga, ka-ga!" Speechless, the Weatherbys turned away from one another and watched the dog and his passenger disappearing together down the hill and heading toward the woods.

When Quincy and Kudzu had reached the safety of the woods, Quincy stopped running and looked back to see if the Weatherbys had decided to chase after them. But the Weatherbys were still standing on the porch and staring in their direction.

"They will never like me, Kudzu," said Quincy.

"Oh, sure they will," said Kudzu.

Quincy lay down to rest and panted to cool himself. "I don't think so," he said. "I wasn't hurting anything or anybody. They just don't like me."

"No," said Kudzu, deciding to lie down across Quincy's back, "the Weatherbys are good people, Quincy. They may do bad things sometimes, but I know them, and they are mostly good. What we have to do is show them that you are mostly good, too, and not mostly bad."

"Good luck!" said Quincy.

"Hey, if I can learn that about you and get to like you, then they can, too. Watch," said Kudzu. He patted Quincy, giving Quincy confidence. "Just watch," Kudzu told him.

Once Quincy had rested long enough, Kudzu said that he knew who would know where they could find the fox. "She's a wise friend of mine," said Kudzu, "who knows how you can find water and everything else, too, I imagine. She's an opossum, and her name is Ophelia. Do you know her?" he asked, but Quincy didn't know any opossums. Unfortunately, like Kudzu, Quincy didn't know where to begin looking for an opossum either. So they decided to hunt for Ophelia the hard way—by wandering through the woods and calling out her name.

They did find the praying mantis that Kudzu had met several days ago. But the mantis, busy eating a moth, had no knowledge of Ophelia's whereabouts. And he had no knowledge of the fox's whereabouts either. Kudzu and Quincy continued on and talked to a turtle and a robin and a skunk and three squirrels, but nobody had any information on Ophelia or the fox.

Kudzu finally told Quincy that they could not afford to waste any more time. There was only one source of information left that they could rely on. So they slowly began the risky journey of making their way back to the farmhouse in broad daylight. They used their combined abilities of seeing and hearing and smelling over long distances, and then Quincy would dart as fast as he could from tree to tree and shrub to shrub, until they finally reached the house without the Weatherbys spotting them.

As before, Kudzu climbed up the cedar stump below the Weatherbys' kitchen. Quincy watched as Kudzu was about to enter the house. "Don't be gone so long this time, okay?"

"I'll be back as soon as I can," Kudzu promised.

"And if you can, bring me back some more cat food," said Quincy. "I'm starving."

"Okay, Quincy," smiled Kudzu. "If I can." Kudzu slipped between the boards and passed through the maze to Stanley's nest of cotton balls, but Stanley wasn't there. In fact, Stanley was nowhere to be found in his home between the walls.

Kudzu knew to look for him in only one other place. He peeked through the hole behind the Weatherbys' refrigerator, and there Stanley was, sitting on folded legs before the screen and listening to Mrs. Weatherby sing as she cooked.

Kudzu cupped his paws around his mouth. "Pssst."

Stanley turned, and when he saw it was Kudzu, he smiled and waved him over.

"I didn't expect to see you again so soon," Stanley whispered, "but I'm glad you came because you won't believe what the Weatherbys are saying about you and your dog friend now."

Kudzu sat down close to Stanley and was amazed at the details that Stanley had to share. After the Weatherbys had seen Kudzu and Quincy run off together into the woods, they had come into the kitchen, laughing about what they'd seen. Mrs. Weatherby had so enjoyed the sight of such an unlikely friendship between a dog and a chipmunk that she immediately got on the telephone to tell her daughter and all her friends about it. Stanley said that he hadn't heard Mrs. Weatherby sing in a long time, but after she finally got off the phone, she began to sing in the kitchen while dicing onions and didn't stop until she'd baked a cake.

Kudzu told Stanley about his plan, but then he asked if Stanley thought the plan would even be necessary. "Maybe the Weatherbys will take Quincy in now," he said, but Stanley shook his head.

"They are amused by you," said Stanley, "but that doesn't

mean they are ready yet to have another pet. That's a long-term responsibility. The Weatherbys never rush into anything like that. You should've heard the debate they had before taking in their cat, Dollop." He continued to shake his head. "No, Kudzu, you've got an excellent plan. I suggest you stick with it."

"Then help us," said Kudzu. "We don't know what a fox print even looks like or where a fox usually lives."

Stanley took off his glasses, looked at them, and breathed warm air on the lenses to clean them. "Coming to me was a good idea," he said, nodding at Kudzu. "I may not know anything about foxes, but I do know where we can find the information you need." He put his glasses back on and told Kudzu about a brand-new knowledge machine two men had delivered to the house just a couple of days ago to help Mr. and Mrs. Weatherby teach Owen what was called "vocabulary." The Weatherbys stored the machine in their living room.

"Really?" said Kudzu, and he sneered, thinking of the red-haired half-reptile man who'd tossed the fire stick into the escape tunnel of his brand-new burrow. "But I thought they were delivering food," he said.

Stanley's long, hairless opossum-like tail rose up from the floor in such a ghostly way that it seemed as if it were the skeleton of a totally separate animal deciding to wake and dance. The tip of the tail curled toward the side of Stanley's head and tapped it. "Food only for the mind, my chipmunk friend," he said. "The machine's called *a computer*, and with a computer you can find everything you would ever want to know."

Kudzu jumped to his feet. "Let's go talk to it then."

Stanley smiled. "That's what I thought at first, too," he said, "but you don't talk to it. You get on it."

"Then let's go get on it!" said Kudzu.

With the tip of his tail, Stanley pointed through the screen at Mrs. Weatherby. "Do you see that human standing there?"

"We can't afford to put this off any longer," Kudzu explained. "I've got a starving dog on my paws, and if I don't get to work soon gathering food for the winter, I'll be starving right along with him."

"And you think we can sneak by Mrs. Weatherby without any problem?" Stanley asked, and Kudzu nodded confidently. "Well, what about *her*?" asked Stanley. "What about Dollop?" Stanley pointed across the kitchen at the slender white cat sitting on the windowsill licking her paws.

"Oh," said Kudzu.

"We can't go in there to get on the computer right this moment," said Stanley. "But we can later tonight, when the Weatherbys go to bed, because when they go to bed, they always take Dollop with them. Nighttime, Kudzu, is the only time we can ever step away from the safety of this refrigerator. So we have to wait. We have no choice."

Kudzu patted the mouse on the back. "Right you are, Stanley," he said. Kudzu turned around to head back toward the hole. "Quincy's outside waiting for me, so I really should go keep him company for a while. Until nighttime anyway." Kudzu took a few steps, then stopped. He was thinking of how Stanley would have to wait by himself. "Would you like to come along?" asked Kudzu.

Stanley grinned and hurried to catch up. "I've been hoping to meet this famous dog," he said, "since I've already met the famous chipmunk."

Kudzu put his arm around Stanley's shoulders. "Believe me," said Kudzu, "Quincy wants to meet the famous mouse, too."

Stanley's eyes beamed with the joyous, bright light that shines only when you know you are someone's friend.

CHAPTER 10

A Mouse Rolls, a Cap Flies, and a Book Knows What it Knows

With each passing day of autumn, the sun seemed to grow sleepier and sleepier. Gradually, it would rise lower in the sky and then go back down sooner than the day before. But on this autumn day in the ancient river valley, the arrival of night seemed to take forever. Especially for a shepherd dog and two rodents waiting underneath the Weatherbys' farmhouse. Even when darkness finally did arrive, there was still much more waiting in store for the two rodents, who had moved inside and were now hiding underneath the Weatherbys' refrigerator. The sun may have already gone to bed, but the many manmade lights burning throughout the house kept the house well-lit for hours.

In this time of make-believe sunlight, Kudzu heard sounds he had never heard before. There were the sounds of a dishwasher, a television, and a rocking chair creaking on a wooden floor. But the strangest sounds of all that he heard came from the Weatherbys themselves, from their very own mouths—when they spoke to one another after they had taken out their dentures. Until Stanley explained what was going on, Kudzu believed he was listening to two entirely different people who had somehow secretly entered the house.

Over the course of the evening, the Weatherbys gradually migrated deeper into their house, first from the kitchen to the living room, and then from the living room, down the hallway, to the guest room and then to the bathroom and then back to the guest room to put a clean Owen to bed before they finally went to their bedroom in the back of the house, with Dollop the cat always closely following. Not long after they shut their bedroom door did they turn the last light out. When Mr. Weatherby began to snore a few minutes later, Stanley whispered to Kudzu to remain very quiet.

As Stanley led Kudzu through a narrow passageway between the refrigerator and a cabinet, Kudzu had the feeling that he was walking through a tunnel and was about to enter someone's burrow. But when they reached the open area of the kitchen, Kudzu no longer felt that he was in anything as familiar to him as a burrow. He had never been in anybody's home this large, where there was so much space. Too much space! Kudzu wondered how the Weatherbys had ever managed to keep invaders out of their home. And by invaders, Kudzu was thinking of prowlers much bigger and more dangerous than a mouse or chipmunk.

Kudzu followed Stanley as he went directly to the cabinet beneath the kitchen sink, which was beneath the window that faced the flowerbed. With his nose and feet, Stanley then pried open the door.

Kudzu was confused. "I thought you said their computer was in the living room."

"Yes," said Stanley, "but their trash can is in here." He climbed in, and he came right back out with a half-eaten cookie. He offered to share it with Kudzu, but eating was the last thing on Kudzu's mind.

"I'm too nervous to eat," said Kudzu, stroking his tail, which was tucked beneath him. "I don't know how you do it."

"That's why I do it," Stanley explained, with a mouth full of cookie. "I always eat when I'm nervous."

When Stanley finished chewing and swallowed, he shut the cabinet door and led Kudzu to the living room. The television and the rocking chair were in this room, and so was the computer, sitting on a desk in the corner. Kudzu watched as Stanley reached the desktop by climbing up one of the electrical cords. It was a slow and difficult task for Stanley, but since Kudzu had longer legs, he was able to reach the desk an easier way. He hopped onto the cushioned seat of the desk chair, hopped from there to the chair's arm, and then, in one step, crossed over to the desk and joined Stanley with a smile.

"Now it's my turn to show off," Stanley said. He went to the volume control knob and turned it all the way down, so as not to wake the Weatherbys with the machine's loud music. Then he was ready to push the start-up button, and the computer turned on in a silent but dazzling display of light and language. What was even more amazing, thought Kudzu, was how Stanley worked the controls by running back and forth, pushing keys on the keyboard and moving around what Stanley proudly called a mouse. In a matter of a few seconds, he had connected them to the Internet, which meant, Stanley explained, that the whole wide world and all its knowledge could be theirs.

"See," said Stanley, and he stood up on the keyboard so that he could underline the number on the screen with a claw, "there are over three million websites on the subject of fox alone."

"But I just need one," said Kudzu.

Stanley shook his head and snickered. "Kudzu, just watch and be amazed."

One by one the websites that Stanley brought up on the screen had nothing to do with foxes and how to find them. Instead, strangely enough, they were about human women or about fur coats for human women to wear, or about posters or paintings of fox hunts that someone could buy at a discounted price. Stanley explained that Kudzu had to be patient, that eventually they would find the information he needed. But Kudzu grew tired of the fancy knowledge machine and wandered to the other side of the desk to look at the books in the nearby case.

There were books of all colors and sizes on the shelves. Some had shiny covers, and some had no covers. Some were thick, and some were thin. Kudzu had never learned how to read, so he had no idea what information might lie within them. What amazed him about the books was how each one came in a completely different package. Sometimes the writing on the outer edge of the book would go across, and then sometimes it would go down. Sometimes a book had a long name, and sometimes it had only a single letter printed on its spine. Sometimes the pages were painted gold on top, while others were blue or red or the color of natural living wood. He noticed also that thin books were usually tall books, and thick books were usually short books. But what he believed he liked most about books was how he could reach out and touch them and open them and even touch the information inside, the words themselves. It was amazing that humans had found a way to capture the breaths of words from thin air and store them on paper.

And that's what Kudzu decided to do. He reached out and touched the books, and surprisingly each book seemed to feel different to him, too. As he ran his paws across them and came upon the books that had a single letter of the alphabet printed on their spines, he was struck with an idea. Based on what Stanley had typed into the computer, Kudzu knew how to spell *fox*, so he pulled out the book titled *F*. And in the book titled *F*, he found what he had been looking for all along. He knew for sure he had found it because of the pictures. There were no silly photographs of human women who didn't even look like real human women, or of fur coats that didn't even look like real fur coats. Only the animal itself was pictured, along with pictures of the animal's home and the animal's paw print.

He called Stanley to come over and read to him what he'd found, and although Stanley didn't want to leave the computer, he finally did. After a moment, Stanley admitted that Kudzu had in fact found exactly what they'd come looking for. But as Stanley read aloud the article from the encyclopedia, Kudzu stopped feeling happy and grew sad.

Kudzu had believed his plan to help Quincy was perfect, but he'd just learned that he'd been mistaken. The fox, the article stated, was a smart and brave animal that could almost always defeat a dog if it was forced to fight in a one-on-one situation. However, as Stanley read on, they learned that in the Southern portion of the United States, it was now the beginning of mating season for foxes.

"Are we in the Southern portion?" asked Kudzu.

Stanley nodded, his eyes still on the words of the article. "So the male and female will be hunting together and protecting each other during this time."

Quincy against a pair of foxes? Kudzu would never allow Quincy to put himself in that kind of danger.

When Stanley reached the end of the article, Kudzu helped

him close the book and put it quietly back on the shelf. Even though they didn't make enough noise for a human to hear, Mr. Weatherby suddenly quit snoring. Stanley motioned for Kudzu not to make a sound or move a muscle, and for a moment, Stanley listened for signs of movement in the Weatherbys' bedroom.

When Stanley heard nothing, he whispered, "Let's shut this ridiculous thing down, so we can hurry up and get out of here." Stanley instantly began the difficult process of working the mouse. He pressed his body against it to make it roll and hopped onto its button to make it click. Then, he repeated the same process again and again.

Kudzu remembered that in the beginning there were buttons and knobs Stanley had turned so that the computer would come on. Kudzu decided he ought to help Stanley, so he went to the first knob Stanley had touched to make everything work. But what Kudzu failed to understand was that this knob didn't need to be touched again. In fact, it should never have been touched again—not until the computer was completely shut down. This was the volume control knob Kudzu had turned on, and now music that played every time a program closed was playing and making a tremendous racket. It sounded to Kudzu as if whole families of crickets, woodpeckers, and bobwhites were making an awful racket to get out of that speaker box.

"No, no!" Stanley shouted. "Cut that off! Kudzu, cut that off!"

But Kudzu was too startled to undo what he had done. Confused and frightened, he accidentally turned the knob the wrong way, and the music blared even louder.

Stanley ran over to the speaker and switched the volume off, then stood very still, holding his breath. This time there was movement back in the Weatherbys' bedroom—human feet moving swiftly across the floor.

"They're coming!" said Stanley, and at that moment, a

doorknob rattled and the hinges of the bedroom door made the whining sound of a mosquito.

Kudzu took Stanley's warning to heart. In one fluid motion, he hopped from the desk to the chair's arm, from the arm to the chair's seat, then from there to the floor. And once he was again on the floor, he looked to see if Stanley was right behind him, but he wasn't. Stanley was still busy working to turn the computer off.

"Hurry up!" shouted Kudzu. He could hear the soft pads of Dollop's paws drumming against the floor of the hallway.

Kudzu then heard Stanley snap a button, and the computer screen suddenly went black. Stanley had finally finished, but in one easy bounce, in one quick blur of white, like a shooting star, the cat had sprung from the floor and onto the desk.

"Watch out!" shouted Kudzu, but Stanley had seen Dollop coming, and Stanley was running for his life. The cat was also running for Stanley's life, and she was much too fast for him. Her legs were too long and strong. And her claws were too sharp. Stanley dove to escape her, which Kudzu didn't understand because Stanley had obviously dove too soon. Stanley wasn't close enough to the edge of the desk to dive for any escape. Stanley appeared to be diving for the computer mouse, as if he had thought the mouse would help protect him. It was a tragic mistake, and Kudzu could not watch any longer. He had to turn away.

By turning away, though, Kudzu missed seeing Stanley's great escape. Stanley had dived for the mouse, and when he landed on the mouse, the mouse flew across the desk much faster than he could have run across it himself, so Stanley missed the cat's claws. But Dollop was springing forward again, and her outstretched claws were gaining on him. Just as Dollop was about to catch Stanley, the mouse rolled right off the edge of the desk and dropped out of sight, carrying Stanley with it. Dollop had no way to stop then, having nothing to grab onto to slow herself down, so she kept going forward and flew headfirst into the bookcase.

Stanley shrieked with terror as he dropped through the air: "Ahhheeeeeeoooooo ahhhhhhhooooooo!"

Hearing this terrifying cry from his friend, Kudzu looked up and saw Stanley alive and surprisingly unhurt, but clinging onto the falling mouse all the same. And then the mouse ran out of computer cord, which jerked the mouse to a stop. Unable to hold on and stop as suddenly as the other mouse, Stanley launched forward.

"I've got you!" yelled Kudzu. He rushed under him with open arms, and as Kudzu caught him, they both tumbled backward. They looked at each other, and once they realized they were lucky to both be unhurt, they scrambled to their paws.

Dollop shook off her dizziness, then hissed as she saw the mouse and chipmunk running toward the kitchen. She quickly sprang after them.

"What do you see, Dollop?" asked Mr. Weatherby. Bracing his shotgun against his shoulder and holding his finger firmly on the trigger, he switched the living room light on with his elbow. When he saw two small shadows darting into the kitchen, he relaxed with relief that it was only mice who had gotten inside. "Go get them, Doll," he laughed.

But Kudzu and Stanley weren't laughing. "Hurry!" called Kudzu. Stanley was a couple of steps behind Kudzu, and Dollop was only a couple of steps behind Stanley.

Kudzu had almost reached the safety of the refrigerator, but he had to think of helping Stanley now, and an idea occurred to him. There was one more use left for his acorn cap. He snatched it from his head and turned around.

"Run!" he told Stanley, and as Stanley ran past, Kudzu let his acorn cap fly. He tossed it with all his effort. The cap spun through the air as Kudzu had hoped it would, and it popped Dollop in the pink triangle of her nose.

It didn't hurt the cat, but it stunned her. She had never

known of a rodent to fire weapons before, and as she considered this new and strange behavior, she slowed down and eventually stopped running altogether to play with the acorn cap that was rolling in a circle on the floor.

Once inside Stanley's home between the walls, Stanley hugged Kudzu and patted him on the back. "Thank you, thank you, thank you!" said Stanley. Then he collapsed onto his nest. He was exhausted but grinning. "Oh, Kudzu," he said, "it's great to still be alive!"

Kudzu was happy for Stanley, but he was not happy for himself just yet. He and Quincy still had to reach the woods before they could consider themselves safe. Mr. Weatherby could be heading outside right now to shoot them with his shotgun.

"Pray we have luck," said Kudzu, and as he hurried away to the cedar stump, Stanley prayed God would grant Kudzu and Quincy much good luck.

"What's going on up there?" asked Quincy.

"I'll tell you later," said Kudzu, hopping from the stump onto Quincy's back. "Let's get out of here!"

Quincy clawed and wiggled his way out from under the house. Then seeing that the coast was clear, he took off for the woods.

Kudzu wondered how he should break the news to Quincy about what he'd learned about foxes. He even wondered if he should tell Quincy anything at all. Knowing his German shepherd pride and stubborn sense of loyalty, Quincy would probably want to risk his life to fight two foxes. Kudzu tried and tried to come up with a new plan he could present to Quincy, one that was better than the first, but he had no ideas. He was absolutely blank. Like the computer, his mind was on, but it wasn't giving him anything he could use.

When they reached the woods, Quincy stopped and asked to hear the details of what had happened in the house. But to give himself a little more time to sort things out, Kudzu said he'd tell him everything once they got to the clearing. Yet after a few minutes had passed, Kudzu still hadn't come up with a new plan. They were already rustling through the undergrowth and approaching the clearing in the woods, and Kudzu then decided he'd just tell Quincy the truth. That's what Quincy deserved.

When Quincy stepped into the clearing under the moonlight, his muscles tensed up, and his ears stood straight. "Look," he told Kudzu, so Kudzu crawled up Quincy's neck and sat on top of Quincy's head, where he saw what Quincy was seeing. On the bed of pine needles underneath the pine tree lay a dead opossum, and beside her, beside the mother, lay six dead young opossums.

"Stay here," Kudzu whispered, and Kudzu dropped to the ground and walked up to the mother opossum. When he saw her up close, a smile stretched across his face. "Hi, Ophelia," he said.

An eye peeked open. Then both eyes looked at Kudzu. She tucked her tongue back in her mouth, and a smile spread across her face. "I should have known it would be you, Kudzu!" She laughed and turned to her children, whose gray hair had begun to grow in like their mother's. "It's okay, young'uns," she said, "you can get up now. It's safe." She rolled over onto her feet, and all six children ran to her and clung to her back, still in fear of the little stranger. "My goodness, Kudzu," Ophelia said, shaking her head at him, "you're sounding louder and bigger in these woods all the time!"

"No," Kudzu corrected, "it wasn't *my* big feet making all that noise this time." He pointed behind him at Quincy standing in the shadows—his eyes glowing in the moonlight. "This time it was his, Quincy's big feet."

Quincy stepped out of the shadows. "Hello," he said.

Seeing the whole enormous height and length of the dog's body, his sharp teeth shining at her from his enormous grin, Ophelia fell flat onto her belly, crumpled up her legs, and stuck her tongue out. She had never met a dog that was ever kind to an opossum. Of course, neither had her children, so they quickly followed their mother's example and began playing dead, too. They held their hands to their hearts. They moaned, and they groaned.

"I'm a goner!" one shouted.

"I love you all," said another.

"Goodbye, cruel world," said yet another.

The young opossums then stumbled from their mother one by one and fell to the ground, but their performance wasn't over. They gasped for air as they crawled across the ground. They coughed, and they choked. Then all at once, they rolled onto their backs, balled their feet into tiny fists, and stuck out their tongues.

Quincy looked at Kudzu, and it was clear by his wrinkled brow and folded ears that Quincy had no idea what had just happened and why. But Kudzu did have an idea. And Ophelia and her children had given it to him. Of course! thought Kudzu. Quincy didn't have to hunt and fight a *real* fox to become a hero and win the Weatherbys' love and respect. Quincy only had to pretend to do that. Quincy only had to *play* the working dog, not *be* the working dog.

Kudzu turned back to admire the seven opossums playing opossum. Kudzu nodded his head with delight. The opossums' game of playing dead to protect themselves from hungry predators was different than other types of games, but it was still a game all the same. And playing games was something Quincy had already proven very capable of doing. That was how Kudzu and Quincy had met in the first place. Didn't Quincy at the time pretend to be such a monstrous predator himself that Kudzu believed he was indeed a monster? Yes, thought Kudzu, continuing to nod his head. This was the best plan yet. If they planted fake fox prints by the chicken coop and Quincy pretended to chase the fox away, then everyone would be a winner. Quincy would have a home, and then he could protect the chickens for real. No one would have to lose, and no one would have to die. Not a fox, or two foxes, and not a dog!

CHAPTER 11

A Pair of Foxes

Once Kudzu had convinced Ophelia and her young ones that they needn't be afraid of Quincy, they soon cheerfully came back to life and continued on their way to find food. It was then that Kudzu asked Quincy to sit, and he shared his new plan with him.

"That's a better plan than your first one," Quincy said, nodding. "It's easier and a whole lot safer, but, Kud," he said, folding his ears and looking troubled, "how in the world will we make fox prints in the dirt without a fox's foot to make them with?"

Kudzu had been waiting for Quincy to ask this very question. He bent down to the ground and brushed away the pine needles before him. Then he scratched in the dirt until he'd made what was very similar to a dog's paw print, with the stamped impression of pads and claw marks, but one that was half the size of Quincy's. The print still didn't look natural yet to Kudzu, though. It wasn't pressed smoothly in the dirt the way Kudzu remembered seeing in the F book in the Weatherbys' bookcase, so Kudzu decided to try something. He patted his nose in the dirt where the scooped-out places were, then he stood back, turned around, and with his tail he lightly swept the area around the print to erase his own paw prints.

Kudzu looked at the make-believe fox print, then at

Quincy. "What do you think?" he asked.

Quincy eased himself down on his belly and crossed his front legs. "It looks like the paw print of something, that's for sure," said Quincy. "Now, I've never seen a fox print before, but if you say that looks like one, then I believe you, Kud. I believe you."

Kudzu rested his chin on his paw as he studied the print in the dirt and compared it to the one he remembered. "Well," he nodded, "that's exactly what it looks like to me."

"Then I believe you," said Quincy. "It looks like the print of something I've never seen, so you must be right. A fox print must look exactly like that."

Kudzu moved closer to Quincy and lay down beside him. Without the warmth of his acorn cap, he could tell that nights were gradually growing colder. Not so cold that Kudzu needed to begin hibernating, but soon he'd have to begin digging a burrow and collecting nuts for the coming winter. Soon Kudzu would have no more time to help Quincy, and he didn't know how long Quincy could survive on his own without help. The success of this latest plan would probably determine whether Quincy lived long or lived short, so before going to sleep this night, Kudzu prayed.

He prayed as his mother had taught him to pray. He respectfully covered his eyes with his front paws, then spoke silently so that only God could hear his words. "Those I love," he prayed, "are in need of your blessing. Please bring them peace on your wind, food with your light, and a long, happy life after this good night."

Kudzu would normally uncover his eyes after saying his prayer, but he decided this time that he would remain in the praying position and go to sleep that way. And all night as he slept, he dreamed of winds blowing through the colorful trees, of the sun warming up the day, and of his best friend smiling, without a worry in the world.

But when Kudzu woke the following morning, he did not find the world the way he'd dreamed. Instead of the sun rising into a blue heaven, there was rain and the sky was gray. And the leaves were not floating on the wind like butterflies. Instead, heavy from the rain, the leaves dropped from the trees like spiders. And then there was poor Quincy. Sitting pressed against the pine tree to escape the rain, he looked more worried about his future than ever before. How could Kudzu now plant fox prints without the rain washing them away?

"Don't worry," Kudzu told him. "Our plan's not ruined yet. The rain can't rain forever." Kudzu stood up and shook the raindrops from his back. "We've got all day to wait, Quincy. And do you know why? Do you know what tonight is?" When Quincy shook his head, Kudzu told him. "Tonight is church night." Kudzu smiled, realizing that tonight was the time God must have wanted them to carry out their plan. Of course, he thought. On church night!

Kudzu proved right. The rain did not rain forever. In fact, it eventually stopped late in the afternoon. Then the clouds started to break apart, and the sky cleared just in time for Kudzu and Quincy to watch another beautiful October sunset unfold before their eyes.

Afterwards, they turned their attention to the Weatherbys inside their house. Kudzu and Quincy hid behind the oak tree with the bird feeders, and while they waited for the Weatherbys to leave, Kudzu searched the ground and found an acorn cap that fit his head just as well as the one before.

Once the Weatherbys had finally stepped outside, strapped

Owen in his car seat, and drove away in their car, Quincy carried Kudzu across the farm to the chicken yard. Near the chicken coop but outside the fenced yard, Kudzu began laying down several leaves that he could walk on and kneel on to keep his paws from making unwanted prints in the mud. Now, he was ready to begin making the fox prints themselves.

He pressed his knuckles and claws and nose in the mud, making a total of eight fake fox prints. Four pointed in the direction of the chicken coop, and four pointed in the opposite direction, so it would appear that Quincy had scared the fox away before it could even cross the fence. Since he found that pressing prints in mud was easier than carving them in dirt, Kudzu decided to plant eight more, so it would appear that a pair of foxes had come and been scared off.

"Now, I'm really going to be a hero," said Quincy. He became so excited by the thought of becoming a hero twice decorated, he took off running. He ran to the pecan orchard, then cut around a tree and ran back to the chicken yard, kicking up mud. "I'm really going to be a hero," he told Kudzu. Then he took off again, this time to the vegetable garden, and he rushed right back. "Kudzu, thank you!" he said. "Quincy, the hero!" he sang. "Yes," he said, "I like the sound of that!"

Kudzu laughed. "Calm down, Quincy. You've got to be careful," he said, holding up his muddy paws to stop Quincy from coming any closer. "We don't want the hero to stomp all over the fox prints, do we?"

"No!" said Quincy, backing far away from them.

"Once the Weatherbys are parked and get out of their car," Kudzu reminded him, "that's when I'll start shouting for you to begin barking. You got that?"

"I got it, Kudzu. I got it, I got it, I got it!" Quincy was so excited about the evening's events that he started to pant and feel he couldn't sit still another second.

"When the Weatherbys come out this way to see what you're barking at," said Kudzu, "start pointing to the prints so they can't miss them, okay?"

Quincy nodded, then showed Kudzu how he'd point, with his nose to the ground and his right front leg hiked up to his chest.

"Excellent!" said Kudzu.

"How long do you think we'll have to wait till they come home?" Quincy asked.

"I don't know." Kudzu had never paid attention to how long the Weatherbys were at church, only that they went and returned.

"Stanley will know, right?" asked Quincy. He was so excited about the evening's events that he started to pant again and feel he couldn't sit still another second.

"Let's go ask him," said Kudzu.

"Let's go, then. Hop on," said Quincy.

Kudzu climbed aboard, and Quincy took off running.

As they approached the house, Quincy began to slow down and grow fearful. He was picking up the scent of exhaust still lingering in the air from a nearby automobile, and of humans nearby, too. Kudzu smelled these same smells.

"Are we too late?" asked Quincy. "Are the Weatherbys back already?"

Before answering, Kudzu hopped on Quincy's head and raised his nose high in the air so he could smell those smells once more. Now, he was sure of it. "Quincy," he said, "that's not how the Weatherbys smell. And look, that's not even their car."

"Maybe Owen's parents have come back to pick him up," said Quincy. "Should I start barking now?"

"No, not yet," said Kudzu. He climbed down to Quincy's back. "Take me around to the garage. Something's not right."

A loud crashing noise of breaking glass suddenly came from the rear of the house, from the back porch—not far from where they stood.

"Wait here," said Kudzu. He leaped to the ground and

scurried to the house to find Stanley, who was shaking with fear and watching everything from underneath the refrigerator.

"Burglars! We've got burglars, Kudzu!" Stanley said. "And look who they are. Just look who they are!"

Kudzu peered through the screen below the refrigerator, and he saw a small man with a billy-goat beard unplugging the cooking machine that the Weatherbys called a microwave. Then, in the living room, there was a second man, a much larger man—the red-haired half-reptile man! The fire-stick man! The sleeves of his flannel shirt were rolled up, showing the same wild pictures drawn all over the muscles of his arms, and in those arms, he carried a wide, black, shiny board, maybe a door, as if the man was planning to steal the whole house, piece by piece.

Stanley gasped. "The T.V.!"

"The T.V.?" Kudzu asked.

"News with Emma Emerson at five and ten," said Stanley.

"Let's get the computer next," the half-reptile man said.

"Of course," the billy-goat man laughed. He lifted the microwave into his arms and followed the half-reptile man out the back door.

A reflex from instinct, Kudzu rapidly chirped his chipmunk warning, but the warning didn't come out of his mouth the way it ever had before, not the way his parents had taught him. It vibrated deep in his throat, like a growl.

"It doesn't make sense," said Stanley.

Kudzu shook his head. "I'll be right back." He ran back through the walls, and he found Quincy waiting for him underneath the house beside the cedar stump.

"What's going on?" said Quincy. "Who's in there? Did you see Stanley?"

Kudzu told him all that he knew, and when he turned to go back inside to see what would happen next, Quincy asked him not to leave.

"I can't sit still while all this is going on," said Quincy. "They're breaking into my future home." He lowered his head for Kudzu to hop on. "Let's find a window and see what else they're up to."

"Good idea."

Following Kudzu's directions, Quincy crept around the house behind the shrubs to the living room windows near the back porch. Quincy then stood up on his hind legs, with Kudzu perched on top of his head, and together they looked in through the parted curtains.

The half-reptile man was piling computer equipment in the arms of the billy-goat man, and when the billy-goat man could carry no more, the half-reptile man loaded the rest in his own arms. Then both men hurried again out the back door.

Quincy dropped down from the window, and he and Kudzu hid behind the shrub while the burglars carried the computer equipment to the long car parked close to the porch with its doors and trunk open.

The burglars stacked the computer equipment in the car, then dashed back inside. Quincy immediately hopped back up to look in the window, but neither the half-reptile man nor the

billy-goat man was anywhere to be seen. But in the hallway leading to the bedrooms, a light turned on.

"Let's go around," said Kudzu, pointing in the direction Quincy needed to go.

When Quincy reached the lighted bedroom windows, he stood up again on his hind legs, and he and Kudzu peeked in. The billy-goat man was pulling open dresser drawers and searching through Mr. Weatherby's clothes, while the half-reptile man was busy stuffing Mrs. Weatherby's jewelry into the wide pockets of his hunter's pants.

"We've got to do something," said Quincy.

"But what?" asked Kudzu. "What can you and I possibly do?"

"This matters," Quincy said, his speech becoming a growl that shook Kudzu sitting atop his head.

Kudzu stroked Quincy's head to calm him, but Quincy couldn't stop now. He was growling with every breath. And Quincy's eyes hardly blinked as they watched the burglars. The half-reptile man was tossing Mrs. Weatherby's empty jewelry boxes on the floor. Then, with one swift motion, he grabbed the top mattress and flung it off the bed.

"Why did he do that?" asked Kudzu.

Quincy didn't know why this man or any man acted so violently, but Quincy did know this breed of man. Quincy's old owner had belonged to this breed. And seeing this breed again up close made Quincy shake with nervous fear, as though he felt in danger of being mistreated again. But that wasn't it at all. He wasn't afraid of what they might do to him. No, Quincy was actually afraid of what he might do to them.

Although Kudzu turned his attention to the billy-goat burglar, who was digging through a box of papers he'd found in the closet, Quincy kept his eyes locked on the larger, more violent one, the half-reptile man, who was now bending down to grab the bottom mattress. And when the half-reptile man had flung that mattress aside, Dollop sprang from her hiding place beneath the bed. She tried to dart past him and escape from the room, but the half-reptile man was quicker, and he kicked her as she went by.

"Get! Get outta here!" the half-reptile man yelled at her, and Dollop landed with a thump against the far wall. He turned to the billy-goat man. "I hate cats."

The billy-goat man chuckled. "Who doesn't?"

Quincy and Kudzu watched Dollop try to stand, but she crumpled back down in a crying, white heap. Feeling Quincy's muscles tighten into knots beneath him, Kudzu leaned over to peer upside down into Quincy's eyes. Kudzu could see the fire that raged in him, and then Quincy bolted into action. Kudzu held onto Quincy's ears as Quincy whipped around the house. Then, in one leap, Quincy soared over the porch steps and charged through the back door. With no time for explanations or apologies, Quincy gave his head a shake, sending Kudzu safely onto the living room sofa.

"Stay back," Quincy told him, and then he rushed down the hall to meet the men.

CHAPTER 12

Dog!

The half-reptile man was swinging his leg back to give Dollop another kick when Quincy introduced himself by flying at him with his lips snarling and mouth wide open. The half-reptile man had no time to react. All he could do was watch Quincy's mouth snap down on his colorful arm.

"Whaaaaaa!" the half-reptile man screamed. "Hey, get this dog off me!" He tried to shake Quincy off his arm, but Quincy only bit down harder and held on.

The billy-goat man ran up behind Quincy and kicked him in the chest with his boot—exactly where Mr. Weatherby had struck him with the hoe. Quincy immediately let go of the half-reptile man's arm, but only so he could charge the billy-goat man now. Seeing Quincy charging, the billy-goat man turned in an attempt to run away, but Quincy caught him by the leg with his teeth. Then Quincy slung his head from side to side to get a tighter grip on the leg. Quincy's jaws now had such a strong lock on the leg that when he continued to sling his head, the billy-goat man lost his balance and fell to the floor.

"Help!" the billy-goat man hollered. But before the half-reptile man had a chance to sneak behind Quincy and kick him, Quincy wheeled around and met the bloody-armed half-reptile man once more and chased him back into a corner. Quincy snapped at him to keep him there. But when he saw that the bloody-legged billy-goat man was trying to stand,

Quincy charged him again and penned him in the closet. Quincy planned to keep this up forever, to keep going back and forth and penning them in the corner and in the closet. But when Quincy turned back to the half-reptile man, he faced a difficult challenge. The two-on-one fight would not be so easy anymore.

The half-reptile man still cradled his injured arm close to his chest, but now in his other hand he was holding one of the boards that had been lying across the bed frame. He whistled at Quincy.

"Come here, pooch," the half-reptile man called in a half-friendly manner. "Come to me, boy."

Quincy crept forward in small steps. He growled and flashed his teeth. He flexed the muscles in his neck, and the hair along his back raised up. Should he attack first, or should he let the half-reptile man swing the board and miss him before making his move? Quincy was trying to decide the best plan of action when he was shocked to see Kudzu run across the floor and hop on the half-reptile man's leg and take a bite.

The half-reptile man looked down to see what was biting him, and Quincy sprang into the air. As hard and as fast as he could, he threw his body against the half-reptile man's chest and knocked him backward. The half-reptile man swung the board as he was falling, but he was off balance and missed. What he did not miss, however, was the iron bed frame, and his head hammered it with a rich and lingering, sweet sound.

Quincy stood his front paws on the half-reptile man's chest and watched his eyes roll backward and close. Quincy could feel the half-reptile man's heart beating beneath his paws, so he knew the half-reptile man was still alive. But this dangerous man was alive in the best possible way. He was locked for now in the deep, dark cage of his own sleep.

"Quincy!" Kudzu shouted, and when Quincy turned around, he expected to see the billy-goat man coming after him, but the billy-goat man was actually limping in the other direction, hurrying across the room, trying to escape. Quincy leaped to catch him, but the billy-goat man had almost reached the doorway.

Then, as if by magic, the door started to close on its own. But the only magic that was being performed was the magic of teamwork—of a cat helping a mouse, who was helping a chipmunk help a dog, who was helping the Weatherbys.

Stanley had come into the room with Kudzu moments earlier, and when Kudzu had rushed to Quincy's side, Stanley had rushed to Dollop's. And Stanley had soothed Dollop with kind words until she purred. Now friends, they moved quickly to shut the door and trap the man. And together they managed to close the door just in time.

As the door shut in his face, the billy-goat man was stunned by what he saw. Standing in the corner now in view, which the door had once hidden, was Mr. Weatherby's shotgun. He could hear Quincy charging at him, and Quincy was almost upon him. So the billy-goat man grabbed the gun and was able to spin around in time to aim it at the fearless flying dog. The billy-goat man had one second to defend himself, maybe even to end the fight.

But the billy-goat man wasted that second by trying to pull a trigger that he couldn't pull. Mr. Weatherby always kept the safety latch on. So all the billy-goat man knew to do, while Quincy's mouth closed around one of his arms, was scream. And when he screamed, he screamed louder than a blue jay and a cat, louder than three pairs of them. He screamed louder than a herd of sheep in a thunderstorm. Louder even than a pen of hungry pigs. In fact, he was screaming just like a grown man who knew he was caught and would soon be punished.

Kudzu joined Quincy and bit the man on one of his ankles. And then Stanley joined in and attacked the man on his other ankle. Before long, the billy-goat man had dropped the gun and was hopping around the room, as though he were stepping on fire. And he was still screaming, of course. He

thought life could get no worse. But then it did.

Dollop had climbed onto a chair, and when the billy-goat man hopped her way, she jumped onto the arm that was slapping at Quincy. Although it pained her to jump and to cling onto the man's arm, she did it and held on tight. Eventually, the billy-goat man was wrestled to the floor by them all. And once that happened, it was over. The billy-goat man had lost. Quincy let go of the arm and went for the man's throat.

Quincy didn't bite down. There was no need for that much violence. He didn't want to kill the billy-goat man. All Quincy wanted to do was pen him down so that the billy-goat man could not escape the punishment he deserved. If Quincy had to growl and hold his teeth against that man's throat and threaten him with greater harm all night long, then that was what he was going to do.

But Quincy didn't have to hold him down all night long. A police siren could now be heard far in the distance, and it was slowly growing closer and louder. But not loud enough yet for a human like the billy-goat man to hear.

"It's a good thing I called 911 when I did," Stanley said, but only Dollop knew what he was talking about.

Dollop curled her tail around Stanley's shoulders, as though her tail were the arm of a good friend. "I'm sorry I've tried so many times to eat you," Dollop told him.

Stanley smiled and pressed his head against her soft tail. "Instinct is a hard thing to overcome," he said. "I forgive you."

"And I'm sorry I hit you in the nose with my acorn cap," Kudzu told Dollop.

"No," she said, "I deserved that."

Stanley, Dollop, and Kudzu, all standing to the side, now turned their attention back to Quincy and the man he controlled.

"You're doing an excellent job there, Quincy," bragged Kudzu, and Quincy wagged his tail.

Out of the corner of his eye, the billy-goat man spotted Quincy's wagging tail. "You really are a good boy, aren't you?" the billy-goat man said calmly to Quincy. "But the police are coming. You hear that siren? So you can let me up now. Let me go turn myself in. I'm getting up to turn myself in now, okay, boy?"

"Grrrrrrrrrrr," said Quincy.

"Or maybe, maybe, maybe I'll stay right here," said the billy-goat man. To stop from seeing the ugly image of himself any longer in the reflection of Quincy's wide black eyes, he shut his own eyes and waited. He understood finally what the four animals had already known. It was over. The police were coming. And he and his sleeping friend were going to jail.

When the siren of a squad car stopped outside the house, the sound of another car braking to a stop could be heard. Stanley, Dollop, and Kudzu knew this second car wasn't a squad car. They recognized the sound of that car's purring, ticking engine, and after tonight, so would Quincy.

"Y'all wait out here till we say it's clear," a male officer said in a voice all of the animals in the bedroom could hear. Once the two police officers entered the house, it wasn't long before they'd made their way down the hall, had thrown open the bedroom door, and had begun to laugh at what they saw.

Mr. Weatherby wanted to see for himself what could possibly have happened to cause the officers to laugh and to laugh like children. So he told Mrs. Weatherby to wait outside, then went in. But Mrs. Weatherby wasn't going to wait outside with Owen and miss a good laugh, so she unstrapped Owen from his car seat and carried him in with her.

When the Weatherbys reached their bedroom, the officers stepped aside to allow them to have a clear view of the two grown men who had been captured by a dog, a chipmunk, a cat, and a mouse. As the Weatherbys stared at what they saw, what they couldn't believe they were seeing, they did not laugh. They couldn't. Nor did they want to. They could not even breathe. They could only stare silently in shock at the animals sitting strangely calm amidst the bedroom's wreckage.

"Will one of you officers of the law *please* stop laughing for one second," the billy-goat man begged, "and get this dog off my neck before he kills me? Somebody! Please!"

Owen, still in Mrs. Weatherby's arms, pointed at Quincy. "Ga!" he said, and Quincy wagged his tail.

"Did you see that, Mama?" asked Mr. Weatherby, looking back and forth between Owen and Quincy.

Mrs. Weatherby chuckled, giving Owen a tighter squeeze. "I did! He's trying to say *dog* by starting at the tail end of the word, isn't he?"

"And it's like that dog knows it," Mr. Weatherby said.

Kudzu wanted the Weatherbys to hear Owen say *ka* and understand why, so he said, "Hi, Owen," but before Owen could answer, Dollop said, "Hi, Owen," and then Stanley said hi to him, too.

"Ka, ta, sss," said Owen, sweeping a hand at Kudzu and then Dollop and then Stanley.

Mr. Weatherby slapped the top of his head as if to catch a hat that was flying away. "Did y'all hear that?" he asked. He pointed at Owen as if he were the wind. "He said a full word! He said *cats*, didn't he?" He turned to Mrs. Weatherby but he also looked at each officer.

"Sounded like *cats* to me," said the female officer.

The male officer nodded. "I only see one cat, but that's beside the point. The boy did say *cats*."

Owen grinned from the attention and pointed again at Quincy. "Ga!"

Quincy wagged his tail again, then growled hot breath on the billy-goat man's neck before letting him go.

"That's a good dog," the female officer said as she took a pair of handcuffs off her belt.

Quincy circled his friends before sitting down beside them. The half-reptile man was slow to wake, slow to rise, but he eventually was led away in handcuffs behind the billy-goat man.

Mrs. Weatherby set Owen on his feet and scooped Dollop into her arms. She held her cat to her heart and talked sweetly to her, while Mr. Weatherby looked around at the enormous mess of the room, and for a long time shook his head.

Owen walked up to Quincy to pat him, and Quincy licked him across the face. Owen squealed with laughter and ran to his grandfather.

Mr. Weatherby took Owen's hand and walked up to Quincy. "So what's your name?" he asked Quincy.

Quincy told him, but Mr. Weatherby didn't quite catch it.

Then an idea struck Kudzu.

"Good," said Kudzu, and Owen said, "Da!"

Kudzu and Owen both giggled.

"Dog," Kudzu said next, and Owen said, "Ga!" Kudzu repeated *good* and then *dog* over and over, speeding up, and so did Owen, until Owen was saying, "Da-ga, da-ga, da-ga," until, finally, he said, "Dog!"

Mr. and Mrs. Weatherby's mouths hung open. Mr. Weatherby looked like he wanted to smile and would if his mouth weren't so heavily weighted by the shock of the moment, but Mrs. Weatherby looked about to cry and hugged Dollop even closer to her heart. Somehow the animals had inspired Owen to speak in full words. *Cats*. Now *dog*!

"You're a good boy after all," Mr. Weatherby said. He stretched out his hand, but before he could stroke Quincy on his head, Quincy caught Mr. Weatherby's hand with his tongue and licked it until Mr. Weatherby began to laugh.

CHAPTER 13

Even the Fish in the Mississippi

Once the police officers finished their reports, they carried the stolen property back into the house, and a tow truck hauled the burglars' car away. Mr. and Mrs. Weatherby thanked the officers and said goodnight, then Owen, standing between his grandparents, shut the door. The Weatherbys expressed a great sigh of relief. Mrs. Weatherby was holding Dollop close to her heart, and Mr. Weatherby was holding Owen's hand. When they all turned around, they found Kudzu and Quincy sitting very still, right in the middle of the kitchen, as if they were honored guests waiting to be fed.

No one appeared to notice that Stanley had slipped back to his safe post beneath the refrigerator, where he was watching the scene unfold through the screen. Stanley was curious what would happen next.

"We should get them some food, I suppose," said Mr. Weatherby, and Mrs. Weatherby nodded in agreement.

Kudzu and Quincy, Dollop and Owen, and therefore Stanley turned their heads to follow Mr. Weatherby as he opened a cabinet and produced two bowls. He filled one with dry cat food, the same kind that spelled *CAT*, then filled one with water from the sink.

"All right," said Mr. Weatherby, "let's go outside." He stacked the bowls on top of one another and walked to the door, snapping his fingers, and Quincy trotted outside, wagging his tail. Kudzu and Owen followed, but Kudzu didn't know if this was a good sign or not.

Mr. Weatherby set the bowls on the ground near the door, then reached for Owen's hand but lingered a moment, standing inside with the door open, smiling as Quincy gulped his food.

"Don't let him eat it all," Mr. Weatherby told Kudzu with a laugh.

"Oh, that's perfectly all right," Kudzu said.

Quincy raised his head briefly, with an expression of bliss on his face, as if his eyes had witnessed heaven. "You sure?"

Kudzu nodded.

Quincy returned to the cat food with great hunger and great happiness. Kudzu smiled at the pleasant sight of Quincy finally getting a good meal.

"Dog," said Owen and smiled. Mr. Weatherby smiled, too, then shut the door.

Once Quincy had eaten all there was to eat, he licked the bowl until the bowl rattled against the other bowl. He licked it until he'd turned the bowl on its side. He licked it until he'd scooted it inch by inch away, until the bowl was far away in the yard. He licked it until his tongue was simply too dry to lick anymore. Then he trotted back for a big sloppy drink of water, really slapping his face with it, his tongue diving deep and pulling out splashes that Kudzu had to dodge to keep from getting drenched.

"Wow!" laughed Kudzu. "Feel better, Quincy?"

Quincy didn't answer. He was sniffing the ground for crumbs.

When Quincy realized there was no more food to eat or lick or find and that he was full anyway, he and Kudzu decided to crawl beneath the house. Where else would they sleep? At least here, they could listen to the Weatherbys' next move. Right now the Weatherbys were still stirring, putting their house back in order. But once that was done, once they had gone to bed and had woken up again tomorrow, what would their next move be? Kudzu could hardly sleep for thinking of the future, not only the coming winter but all the seasons to come in their lives. Quincy, however, slept more deeply, more soundly, more proudly than Kudzu could remember ever seeing anyone sleep.

It was late when the Weatherbys finally settled down, putting Owen to bed and going to their own bedroom. Not long afterward, Stanley tiptoed out to the cedar stump.

"Good night," Stanley whispered.

"Good night," Kudzu whispered.

Stanley smiled. He glanced at Quincy, twitching in his sleep, then looked at Kudzu again. "Thank you," he whispered.

Kudzu smiled. "You're welcome," he said out of habit, but he didn't understand why Stanley was thanking him. Before he could ask Stanley to explain, Stanley drifted back into the shadows of the house.

It was nice to be thanked, even if Kudzu didn't understand why. He quickly fell asleep.

But his sleep was short and not altogether very restful. Suddenly it was dawn, the rooster was crowing, and Kudzu was still tired. After a series of creaks from the floorboards, the garage door began to move upward with a humming and a crunching. He knew what that meant. Soon Mr. Weatherby would be passing by with a tin bucket of chicken feed, which he stored in the garage.

The noise of the garage door must have woken Quincy. He stretched his legs and yawned, and when his eyes rolled slowly open, there was Kudzu looking back at him. Quincy's tail thumped the ground.

"Good morning," said Kudzu.

"Morning," slurred Quincy, smiling dreamily.

"Mr. Weatherby is up," said Kudzu, and just then he saw Mr. Weatherby approaching alone. "See?" he said, and Quincy rolled over in the other direction to see Mr. Weatherby for himself.

Quincy's eyes turned sad. "Where's Owen?"

"They're probably letting him sleep in," said Kudzu. "Let's go say hello."

Quincy's eyes turned happy again. "Good idea."

Mr. Weatherby was quietly admiring his farm, how first light barely lit the outlines of things—the trees and fences and his rooster perched on his favorite fence post. Then, he must have heard the beat of paws because he turned around. He laughed at the sight of Kudzu riding up on the back of Quincy. That was something Mr. Weatherby believed he'd never get used to seeing. He hoped he wouldn't, anyway.

He patted Quincy and Kudzu each on the head, then continued on to the chicken yard, with Quincy and Kudzu following.

"If only you two could guard my chickens the way you guard my house," said Mr. Weatherby. "Oh my goodness, yes," he said to himself, and he reached for the chain to open the gate.

Kudzu whispered in Quincy's ear, and then Quincy started to bark.

When Mr. Weatherby turned back around to see what the barking was about, Quincy tucked his pointing paw to his chest and aimed his nose at the fox prints that Kudzu had made in the mud the night before.

"What is it, boy?" asked Mr. Weatherby. "What do you see?" He walked over to the strip of mud alongside the fence and saw for himself what Quincy was pointing at. But Mr. Weatherby saw more than fox prints in the mud. Much more. He saw then how truly smart and gifted this dog was.

"Good boy!" Mr. Weatherby cheered. He leaned down and hugged Quincy around the neck. "Good boy!" he repeated.

Quincy licked his face, and Mr. Weatherby laughed.

"You need a good home, don't you?" said Mr. Weatherby.

Quincy licked Mr. Weatherby's face with the hunger of his heart, as if Mr. Weatherby's face were the bottom of a food bowl.

"All right," said Mr. Weatherby, pulling back. He laughed. "All right," he said. He stood back and lifted the chain from the bent nail, then closed the gate quickly behind him, hanging the chain on the nail again. "You have to stay out there," he told Quincy.

Quincy nodded. He didn't mind. He sat and waited patiently while Mr. Weatherby went inside the chicken coop and while Kudzu climbed down Quincy's back to sit beside him.

"Thanks!" said the rooster.

Quincy and Kudzu turned in surprise to hear the rooster speak. "You're welcome," they said and turned to each other with a smile of wonderment. The rooster sucked in a deep breath—his chest rounded with so much air it seemed he might rise up off his fence post and fly away. And then he trumpeted his morning song much louder and more clearly than he ever had before. Far in the distance even the fish in the Mississippi River paused in their swimming to listen.

"Wow!" Kudzu and Quincy chimed together, their ears flared back.

Mr. Weatherby returned from the chicken coop with his bucket, no longer filled with feed but now with the eggs he'd collected. He was smiling as before, as if his smile had become permanent. He opened the gate, then hung the chain on the nail again. He leaned over and patted Quincy on the head. "Yes," he said, "you deserve a good home. Yes, indeed."

"*This* home?" Quincy asked Mr. Weatherby. Quincy looked at Kudzu. "When he says *home*, does he mean *his* home? Will this farm be my *good home*?"

Kudzu shrugged. "Surely," he said.

Mr. Weatherby started walking toward the house, so Kudzu hopped on Quincy's back, and they followed.

"He's giving me *his* home, right?" asked Quincy. "That's what he means, don't you think?"

"I hope so," said Kudzu.

Mr. Weatherby stopped to collect Quincy's empty food bowl, then went inside the house without saying why. He was inside a long time—probably sipping his steaming cup of mud, Kudzu guessed at first. But Mr. Weatherby was inside for so long that it seemed he would never again come out.

"I thought he was bringing me more food," said Quincy. He stretched out on the ground, rested his head on his paws, and sighed.

"I don't think so," said Kudzu. He walked over to the water bowl, stood up on his hind legs, and lowered his head over the edge to take a drink.

Kudzu was so enjoying the water that he didn't even hear the approaching footsteps. The door swung open, and suddenly Mr. and Mrs. Weatherby and Owen were watching Kudzu drink.

Kudzu raised his head, with water dripping from his chin. Behind him, Quincy's tail thumped the ground.

"Well, that's a picture," laughed Mrs. Weatherby.

"I'm telling you!" said Mr. Weatherby. He walked past, carrying a jingling ring of keys.

Owen started to follow, but Mrs. Weatherby caught him.

"Whoa, you're staying with me," she told him.

"No!" Owen said, looking either about to cry or stomp his feet.

"We'll do something fun here together," said Mrs. Weatherby. "We'll play on the computer."

Owen smiled and turned to his grandfather. "Bye-bye," he said, waving, and his grandfather smiled and waved back.

"Get us a cold drink, will you, please?" asked Mrs. Weatherby.

"Will do," said Mr. Weatherby.

Mrs. Weatherby led Owen inside the house and shut the door, while Mr. Weatherby walked to the garage. Kudzu and Quincy stayed on the porch and watched him sit behind the wheel of his old work truck. He cranked it the way it always cranked—after a high-pitched spinning sound that resembled a police siren. Then the truck's engine rumbled and bubbled, and Mr. Weatherby backed the truck out of the garage and then stopped for some reason.

He opened his door, got out, and walked to the rear of his truck. He dropped the tailgate and looked back toward Quincy and Kudzu, or maybe he was looking at the door of the house and was thinking about Mrs. Weatherby or Owen. Then he patted the tailgate. "Come on, boy," he said. "You're coming with me."

Quincy turned to Kudzu with an expression that suggested he was unsure of the situation. Kudzu offered the same expression back.

"Where is he going?" asked Quincy.

"I don't know," said Kudzu.

"Should I go?" asked Quincy.

"I guess you have to if you want to live here." Kudzu shrugged, then hopped onto Quincy's back. "We'll go together."

Mr. Weatherby whistled. "Come on, boy," he said again and clapped his hands.

"Are you holding on?" asked Quincy.

"I'm holding on," said Kudzu.

This wasn't Quincy's first time to jump into the back of a pick-up. Quincy liked jumping into the back of pick-ups. He liked the wind and liked to lick the wind. And thinking of the wind, of motion and speed and blurred objects and blurred colors and blurred sounds and blurred smells, of everything running together as one, he took off running with such a jolt that Kudzu's hind legs were lifted into the air behind him. And with such a good start, Quincy had no problem leaping into the back of the truck. His only problem was stopping. When he landed, he slid on all paws to the other side of the truck bed and bumped against the cab window, making Kudzu laugh a loud chipmunk laugh that Mr. Weatherby thought sounded almost human, making him laugh as well—just like an old chipmunk, thought Kudzu.

"Good boys!" said Mr. Weatherby. He shut the tailgate. "Good boys!"

A blur of black and orange appeared out of the corner of Kudzu's eye, and he stopped laughing.

"Hello, Victoria," said Kudzu.

Before seeing her, just hearing her name, Quincy growled.

Victoria then hovered in full view before them. "I regret that there were misunderstandings before," she said. "That is why I am here this fine morning begging for reciprocity."

"*Reciprocity*?" asked Kudzu.

At the sound of such a complex word, Quincy growled again.

"Yes, *reciprocity*," she said. "Consider, young Kudzu, how my exquisite wings work in harmony to keep me afloat. That's reciprocity. So, from now on, we'll help each other, as if each of us is a wing that helps keep all of us on this farm afloat. How does that sound?"

"That sounds fair to me," said Kudzu.

"You will help me, and I will help you." She rolled her eyes at Quincy. "And you, too, I suppose." She smiled. "Agreed?"

"It doesn't sound like something we should have to agree to," said Kudzu, "but, sure. Agreed." He looked at Quincy. "Well?"

Quincy lifted his shoulders. "I guess, whatever," he said.

"Splendid," she said.

Mr. Weatherby shifted the gears of his truck, and they began to move.

"Let's start with your helping *me*," said Victoria, her wings fluttering faster to stay with them. "I would like a cold drink, too. A bottle of Gatorade, please. You'll know it by the orange lightning bolt on the bottle and its orange cap. That should be easy to remember—orange like me!" She began to fall back as the truck sped up. "That is," she said, raising her voice, "if you manage to make it back!"

CHAPTER 14

Snake on a Stick

Quincy hooked his head over the side of Mr. Weatherby's truck, and the roaring, rushing wind of the road pulled his lips apart, making his eyes bulge. Because Kudzu was clinging onto Quincy, Kudzu was also clinging onto his acorn cap.

"You smell that?" shouted Quincy.

"Yeah," said Kudzu, struggling to speak, the wind filling his mouth. "Yeah. Yeah!" he said louder and louder. It was as if the whole wide world was coming alive at once in his tiny nose.

The whole wide world was bound to include familiar smells, even a smell from his treasured past, and as soon as he caught the smell of a kudzu patch, Kudzu saw the leafy greenery flash by in a blur. He turned to look behind them, and he saw the patch clearly, the remains of his old home, locked between a strip of bulldozed red earth and a meadow.

For a moment the truck slowed, giving Kudzu's eyes a chance to focus and for him to remember growing up, and to remember his sad return to the kudzu patch with Quincy only days ago, which seemed now so long ago. The truck went around a bend in the new black road of progress, and the kudzu patch disappeared from sight.

The truck traveled down the road for a long time before Quincy ducked out of the wind to ask Kudzu how long he thought they'd been driving. But Kudzu didn't know. He looked up at the sun, which hadn't moved much across the sky, but he knew very well they had traveled far. When he thought back on all the birds and flowers and cars and dogs and tractors and houses and creeks and fences and kudzu patches he'd seen in passing, how could they not have traveled far?

Quincy suddenly darted to hook his head over the other side of the truck, and he watched a street and a street sign pass. Kudzu could feel the hair along Quincy's back stand on end and become prickly.

"That was it," Quincy said.

"That was what?" asked Kudzu.

Quincy sat and hung his head out of the wind. "Quincy Street."

"Where you used to live?" asked Kudzu.

Quincy nodded. "What does that mean that we've come a long way?"

Kudzu didn't have an answer.

"I've heard of people driving long distances just to abandon a dog that they don't want."

"Oh, who would do that?" asked Kudzu.

Quincy's eyes drooped. "Lots of people, Kudzu. Lots of people."

"But why?" asked Kudzu.

"So we don't find our way back. Ever."

Mr. Weatherby didn't seem to be the type of man to do such a thing. But Kudzu had been wrong before. He'd never seen the chipmunk trap coming.

"Well," said Kudzu, patting Quincy on the head, "if that's the worst that can happen, we'll be fine. We'll manage."

Quincy shook his head. "That's not the worst, though," he said. "There's always the pound."

Kudzu had never heard of the pound before. Quincy had to explain to him that the pound was where homeless animals were caged. "There's a brief time limit for each one," he told Kudzu, "and if nobody has adopted you when the time is up, your time is up...*forever!*"

Kudzu wished he had never heard of the pound before. He preferred to believe that humans, most of them anyway, were as kind as he and Quincy were. That humans wouldn't want to harm or kill any living thing unless it was to eat or to defend themselves—for survival alone, for no other reason, absolutely none, and even then they wouldn't want to. But maybe all humans deep down inside were cold-blooded and unreasonable, like the half-reptile man or the billy-goat man. Humans could be so very unpredictable.

Even though Kudzu and Quincy were both lost in thought, they both lifted their noses at once to a strange mixture of scents and temperatures circling them. Quincy had smelled this stormy smell before—it was of wood-burning smoke and gas-burning smoke and steam and oil and lumber and bread and spices and tar, and of cars and cars and more cars.

Quincy stood up with Kudzu on his back, and over the side of the truck, Kudzu saw for the first time what was called a town. There were as many people everywhere as there were animals in a forest and as many buildings as there were trees in a forest. Kudzu watched the busyness, the constant labor of fall. They obviously knew winter was coming.

The truck began to slow and then slow some more and then turn and then turn some more and then stop between two white lines.

"This is too familiar, too familiar," said Quincy. He paced nervously from one side of the truck to the other. It smelled more like chicken on one side and more like pine sap on the other, but Quincy knew there had to be something in the middle, something he was missing. He decided to hop up, landing his front paws on the roof of the cab so that he could see what was in front of the truck. So that he could see what Mr. Weatherby was seeing. And he saw it. He saw it.

"Oh, no," said Quincy.

"What?" asked Kudzu. He was seeing what Quincy was seeing, yet somehow he wasn't. All he saw was a building like so many others they'd passed. But then he smelled dog, and he smelled cat. And he smelled something very similar to the blue liquid that Mrs. Weatherby sprayed on the porch windows when she cleaned them.

"The snake-on-a-stick place!" moaned Quincy.

"Where?" asked Kudzu. He scanned the area for snakes and sticks but didn't see any on the ground, and he didn't see any snakes wrapped around the lamp poles between the cars or on the door handles on the building or around the columns by the doors. And then, yes, he did see one. Way up, above the roof of the building, on a white sign bigger than the moon, there was indeed a snake on a stick.

Quincy shook his head, and then his whole body began to shake and shiver. "This could be worse—this could be worse than the pound!"

"What is?" Kudzu looked again at the sign, at the snake on the stick. There was no clue anywhere as to what that meant, at least that he could understand. "What is this place?" he asked.

"The *vet*," Quincy whispered. "Oh, no, the *vet*!"

Mr. Weatherby opened his door, and the weight of the truck shifted as he stepped out.

"What's the vet?" asked Kudzu. "Hurry, tell me. We don't have much time!"

Mr. Weatherby peered with a grin into the back of the truck, and all Kudzu could think of was that they were out of time, that their time was up...forever!

"You two are something else," said Mr. Weatherby.

"Something else?" wondered Kudzu. What did that mean? He didn't want to be something else! He burrowed the tips of his claws into Quincy's thick fur until he finally reached Quincy's skin, hoping to wake him to action. "So what do we do?" shouted Kudzu. "Come on, Quincy, tell me!"

But brave Quincy was a shivering wreck. He opened his mouth, but he could barely speak. "You'll see," was all he could say.

Mr. Weatherby dropped the tailgate, then patted it with the palm of his hand. "Let's go, fella."

Quincy crawled obediently to him, as if he were too scared not to, and Kudzu, as Quincy's best friend, clung obediently to Quincy. But Kudzu squeezed his eyes shut. Maybe he could pass through the snake-on-a-stick place and never see it.

Quincy's claws clicked and scraped across the pavement, and Kudzu squeezed and squeezed his eyes and held on. But it may have been more frightening to enter a foreign place this way, without seeing what was coming. So once the door opened like an enormous mouth sucking them into its colder climate, as if they were deep down now in the pit of winter's stomach, Kudzu couldn't keep his eyes squeezed shut any longer.

He didn't see snakes with icicle fangs hiding among stacks of sticks under snow drifts. He saw only what he should have expected to see if he had trusted his nose: a room full of dogs and cats. They were all shivering like Quincy. All speechless like Quincy. But unlike Quincy, all were either trapped in a cage, especially the cats, or tied by the neck, such as the dogs, and the leashes were twisted around the hands of human owners, who all looked as nice as Mr. Weatherby. And the floor? It was just a floor. Not the lining of a stomach whatsoever!

Everyone, humans and animals alike, turned at once to look at Quincy and Kudzu entering the room. The dogs and cats had sad, sympathetic eyes, some with sick eyes, while the owners smiled and laughed, and that made the snake-on-a-stick place seem weird to Kudzu. More weird really than scary.

A young lady standing behind a desk in bright pink clothes greeted Mr. Weatherby and quickly handed him a leash to loop around Quincy's neck. She asked how she could help him today, and Kudzu and Quincy listened very carefully.

"This stray dog here seems to believe I'm going to give him a home," said Mr. Weatherby. "If so, he needs to be caught up on his shots."

"Shots?" asked Kudzu.

"I knew it!" said Quincy.

"Last night he protected the wife and me from burglars, two of them," said Mr. Weatherby.

"How about that!" the lady said.

Mr. Weatherby nodded at Quincy. "He really did. And since he sank his teeth into them, I guess I ought to make sure he doesn't have rabies."

The lady on the other side of the desk laughed for some reason, and so did the humans seated around the room.

"This is a very weird place," whispered Kudzu.

"The worst!" said Quincy.

"And what about his little friend?" the lady asked. She and

Mr. Weatherby looked directly at Kudzu, and Kudzu froze.

He stopped breathing. His eyes stopped blinking. And if his heart was still beating, he couldn't tell. He was a scared rock.

"Oh," laughed Mr. Weatherby, "he's just along for the ride."

When the other humans joined Mr. Weatherby in his laughter, Kudzu began to shake. He was shaking on top of shaking Quincy. He looked around at all the other shaking animals in the room, breeds he'd never seen before, and none of them appeared to understand the laughter inside this very weird place either.

"Here," the lady said, handing Mr. Weatherby a piece of paper and a pen, "fill this out please while you wait."

Mr. Weatherby took the paper and the pen, then led Quincy by the leash to a chair and sat down.

Beside Mr. Weatherby sat a woman with blonde hair pulled back in a ponytail. She wore blue jeans and a denim jacket, and on the floor at her feet lay a female greyhound with bashful brown eyes and long lashes.

"Hi," said Quincy, trying his best to sound calm.

The greyhound smiled politely, turned her eyes away, and continued shaking like the rest of them.

Quincy had never seen this breed of dog before either. She was...he didn't have the words to describe the shape or clear lines of her head and neck, her whole body. She was almost mushroom-like, with her short, smooth coat, which was a swirl of black and brown from her nose to the tip of her long rope of a tail. She was...different? Interesting? Pretty to look at? He wasn't sure what words to use to describe how she made him feel beneath his skin, far below his shivering. It was as if Kudzu had rubbed off on him and now Quincy had a warm burrow deep inside him that he had just discovered.

"I don't always shake like this, you know," Quincy told her.

"Oh, you think I do?" came the deep voice of the nearby Rottweiler, spitting as he spoke.

"And you think I do?" said the bear-sized Chow Chow. "Come on, dude!"

"Until today," chattered the Chihuahua, sitting perched on a pillow in his owner's lap, "I didn't even know I could shake."

The enormous Rottweiler and the thick-necked chow both rolled their eyes and looked back at Quincy and at Kudzu riding him. The chow licked his lips with a black tongue.

"What sort of dog makes peace with a chipmunk?" asked the Rottweiler. He grinned at the greyhound and flexed his muscles.

"Not much of one," said the chow.

"Any other time, any other place," said the Rottweiler, "I would've already picked a fight with shepherd boy here."

"You would've had to get in line, amigo," said the Chihuahua.

The greyhound turned her eyes to Quincy and Kudzu. "I think they're cute together," she said.

Quincy stared dreamily at her. He was speechless again.

Kudzu removed his acorn cap. "Thank you very much," he said with a bow.

"You know, I used to love chasing rabbits," the greyhound said, speaking to Quincy and only to Quincy, as if he were the only dog in the room. "I chased them all the time, and people bet a lot of money that I could do it faster than anyone else. But once, when I wasn't the fastest, I was whipped with my leash for losing, and then it struck me—what's the sense of winning if someone has to lose?"

Quincy folded his ears and nodded.

"Give me a break!" said the Rottweiler.

The chow and the Chihuahua laughed.

Quincy sneered. "Ignore them," he told her, and the greyhound continued as if she hadn't heard the other dogs at all.

"I hadn't realized that when I was winning," she said, "others were getting whipped for losing, too. So I made a decision to quit chasing rabbits. I simply refused."

"Good for you," said Kudzu.

"Oh, brother!" said the chow.

"I think I'm going to throw up!" the Rottweiler grumbled.

"Get in line," the Chihuahua snapped.

"It wasn't easy to quit," said the greyhound, still completely ignoring them. "My owners became furious with me and whipped me some more. In fact, they were about to have me destroyed when this nice person stepped in and adopted me. She saved my life!" She raised her head to see her owner, and her owner gently stroked her head. The greyhound smiled. "She doesn't mind I'm a racing dog that doesn't race. So I imagine if I had the opportunity to meet a rabbit, then we'd become friends, too."

Kudzu whispered into Quincy's ear.

"You know," said Quincy, "that sounds like *exquisite reciprocity*."

"Yes!" said the greyhound, blinking her eyes and her long lashes. "Yes, exactly! Exquisite reciprocity!"

Quincy nodded with great pride. "My name's Quincy," he

said. "And my little friend is Kudzu."

"Hi, Quincy, Kudzu," she said. "I'm," she said, hesitating, "Two Mississippi."

"Two Mississippi?" Quincy repeated.

"That's a nice name," said Kudzu.

Two Mississippi rolled her eyes. "It's a typical silly racing name."

"No," said Quincy, "it's different. It's interesting and pretty." He hesitated, then asked, "But why *Two* Mississippi? Why not *One* Mississippi?"

She shrugged. "I'm the offspring of One Mississippi."

"Oh," said Quincy, embarrassed to be talking with a female about such science. He smiled shyly and turned away to see the lady behind the desk no longer behind the desk. The lady stepped into the room as she opened a door.

"Two Mississippi!" the lady announced, and Two Mississippi and her owner both stood up.

"It was very nice meeting you two," Two Mississippi told Quincy and Kudzu.

"Yes, very nice," said Kudzu.

"Yes," said Quincy, rising to his paws to see her off. "Good luck!"

Two Mississippi tucked her tail between her legs and trotted in long strides behind her owner across the room and into another room, behind the closing door.

"How very nice!" slobbered the Rottweiler.

"Any other time, any other place," the Chihuahua told Quincy, "you would be all mine!"

Kudzu laughed. "Are you kidding! One more squeak from you and I'm hopping up on that pillow and taking you out myself!"

The Rottweiler and the chow both laughed at the Chihuahua, who curled up on the pillow and looked the other way.

“And that goes for the both of you,” said Quincy, losing his shakes. He stood firm and leaned forward, shifting his eyes back and forth from the Rottweiler to the chow. “I can take two, just try me.”

“Satan!” the lady behind the desk announced, standing again at the open door.

The Rottweiler stood up and grinned at Quincy. “Lucky for you! Just in time!”

“Whatever,” said Quincy. He stood his ground as Satan the Rottweiler and his owner passed by. “See what I mean about that name, Kudzu?”

“I do,” said Kudzu, “but it fits him. Not *you*, Quincy. Not you at all.”

CHAPTER 15

Orange Lightning

It seemed to Kudzu that the worst thing about the snake-on-a-stick place was the wait. But that made it like everything else in life. The wait to eat. The wait to play. The wait to grow up. The wait to meet your next new friend.

Once Mr. Weatherby's name was called and a woman in a long white coat appeared, time flew. The woman in the long white coat lifted Quincy, with Kudzu on his back, onto a silver table. She looked into Quincy's eyes, inside his ears and nose and mouth, and then she inserted a stick in Quincy's behind. Well, Kudzu couldn't watch that.

"What in the world is she doing?" Kudzu whispered.

"I don't know!" Quincy moaned. "I told you this place was the worst."

"You did!" said Kudzu. "You certainly did!"

"Just wait," said Quincy. "It's about to get worse."

"Worse than that?" Kudzu held onto his cap. He thought he might faint.

The woman in the long white coat stepped away and stood at a counter with glass jars filled with items that resembled what Kudzu might find back on the farm—cocoons, sticks, and even dirt clods, which seemed to have the faintest scent of meat, almost like cat food. The woman stood with her back to them for so long that Kudzu thought the woman might turn around with a steaming cup of mud made from one of the dirt clods. But it was worse, way worse. When she turned around, she held in her hand the longest, the sharpest, the shiniest proboscis Kudzu had ever seen. It was hundreds of times larger than any mosquito proboscis or any butterfly proboscis! Kudzu had never seen one attached to the hand and not the mouth! But it certainly was a proboscis, with a tube for drawing nectar or blood, or for injecting poison, and this one was filled. It was filled with what else? Poison!

"Oh, Kudzu," moaned Quincy.

"What, Quincy? Tell me! What's about to happen? What should I do?"

"What do you mean?" asked Quincy.

"I mean, what will happen?" asked Kudzu. "Will you get sick from it? Will you die?"

"Oh, no, nothing like that," said Quincy.

"Then what?" asked Kudzu.

"It's just scary," said Quincy. "Look, just look at that enormous thing!"

Kudzu was confused. He sat with his front paws ready to cover his eyes and watched the woman in the long white coat pinch a fold of skin from Quincy's hind leg and stick him with her hand-held proboscis. Then he watched the woman use her opossum-like opposable thumb to inject Quincy, and Quincy had been right. Nothing happened. Then the woman removed the proboscis and rubbed Quincy's skin as if to soothe it.

"There you go, boy," smiled the woman in the long white coat. "All done. The picture of health."

"Thank you, Doc," said Mr. Weatherby.

"Oh, I almost forgot!" said the woman in the long white coat. She removed the lid from the jar of dirt clods. She took two out and then covered the jar again. "Here you go, for later if you like."

"Nice," nodded Mr. Weatherby.

And that was it. The woman in the long white coat carried

Quincy, with Kudzu, off the table and set him back on the floor.

Quincy wagged his tail and darted for the door, waiting for it to open so he could leave. He sniffed the door. "This is the right way, I know it!" he said. "I know it! It's over, Kudzu! I can't believe it! It's over! We can go now!"

"*Where*?" said Kudzu.

Quincy danced in circles as if he were dancing to music only he could hear. When the woman in the long white coat opened the door, Quincy shot through it and didn't stop running until he'd reached the next door, and he immediately started sniffing that one.

Kudzu removed his acorn cap to scratch his head. "So why is this place the worst place of all?"

But Quincy was too happy to be leaving to be able to answer him. He danced and danced and sniffed the door, then danced some more. He was the happiest Kudzu had ever seen him.

"You can't leave us yet," the lady behind the desk told Quincy. She bent down on one knee and buckled a collar around his neck. On the collar hung a small silver bone-shaped tag that jingled. When she was done, she clipped a leash to the collar and stood up and patted Quincy and Kudzu on the head. She laughed and looked at Mr. Weatherby. "Whenever you have a name for him," she said, "please call and let us know, so we can add it to your file."

"Oh, yes, of course," said Mr. Weatherby. "Thank you so much!"

"Did you hear that, Quincy?" asked Kudzu. "He wants to come up with a name. He's going to keep you!"

But Quincy wasn't thinking of any place so distant as home. He was thinking only of being on the other side of this door, as if he were in a race to get there. And wasn't that interesting, thought Kudzu. Today Quincy had become a non-racing dog that raced!

As soon as Mr. Weatherby pushed the door open, Quincy

bolted forward, almost pulling Mr. Weatherby over. Then, just as suddenly, Quincy stopped at the first blade of grass sprouting between cracks in the concrete and hiked his leg.

"You've got to be careful, Quincy," said Kudzu. "You don't want to hurt Mr. Weatherby."

"Hurt him?" asked Quincy, lowering his leg. "Never!"

"Quincy," said Kudzu, "you almost made him fall. Don't forget you're on a leash now, and he's an old man. Don't hurt him."

"Oh, yes, of course," said Quincy, hardly believing it was true, but if Kudzu said it was true, then it must have been. He turned to look at Mr. Weatherby, whose eyes were a little dazed, and he was a little out of breath. "I'm sorry, very sorry, Mr. Weatherby," he said, knowing Mr. Weatherby would never hear him or understand, but hearing himself apologize always made Quincy feel better about himself.

For added measure, he walked over and licked Mr. Weatherby's hand until Mr. Weatherby smiled. After that, Quincy calmly walked onto the truck and hopped in.

"All right," said Mr. Weatherby, shutting the tailgate, "let me put my purchase order in next door, and I'll be back as soon as I can. Be a good boy now, and stay put," he said, speaking naturally to Quincy, as if he knew Quincy could hear him and understand.

Quincy and Kudzu looked at one another, then watched Mr. Weatherby stroll to the large barn-like building next door that smelled of pine sap.

"What do you think he's ordering?" asked Kudzu.

"I don't know," said Quincy, watching after Mr. Weatherby with concerned eyes. "Do you think he's purchasing an order or looking for someone to purchase his order? You know, maybe he's looking to sell his order to someone who wants a dog with all his shots. You know, who's the picture of health!"

"Oh, no, he likes you, Quincy," said Kudzu.

"You think?"

"It's clear to me, more and more," said Kudzu.

Quincy smiled. "You really think so? To keep me for himself?"

Kudzu nodded. "I do."

"I hope so," said Quincy. He turned his attention back to the building that smelled of pine sap. Mr. Weatherby was no longer in sight.

"Do you think they sell other things in there besides dogs?" asked Kudzu.

Quincy spun around with a frightful expression.

"Quincy, I'm kidding," laughed Kudzu. He hopped from Quincy's back onto the cab of the truck. "Now, be a good boy and stay put," he said.

"Where are you going?" asked Quincy.

"To see if I can make Victoria happy with me," said Kudzu. Maybe if he took a bottle of Gatorade back to her, she would feel she owed him friendship and nothing else. That's what he wanted most of all on the farm. Friendship and nothing else.

Kudzu slid down the windshield, and Quincy stood up on his hind legs to watch Kudzu crawl over the hood, drop down onto the bumper, and then hop to the ground.

"Shouldn't I go with you?" asked Quincy.

"No, the humans will see you," said Kudzu. "Maybe like Stanley I can sneak in and they won't see me."

"Well, okay. Be careful, Kudzu!" Quincy called after him.

Kudzu scurried between parked cars, then hiding under the last one that was closest to the building, he watched the doors magically open on their own whenever someone walked up. And whenever someone inside walked up to the doors to leave the pine-sap building, the doors magically opened again. If Kudzu got in, at least he knew he could get out.

Kudzu took a deep breath and ran for it. When he reached the doors, they magically opened, even for a chipmunk, and it was amazing what he saw inside! It was like Stanley's space between the walls but thousands of times bigger than that, if not millions. Stacks and stacks of stuff all over. Screws and nails and bolts of all lengths and widths. And tools and paints and lumber and flowers. Even feed. Feed for chickens and for cats and for birds—he recognized those. But there was feed also for other animals. For dogs and chipmunks, surely! There were so many items that people went by with baskets and took whatever they wanted.

There seemed to be everything anyone might want except for only two things: acorns and Gatorade. Luckily for someone like Kudzu, you could collect your own acorns. But for someone like Victoria, you were out of luck.

He discovered Mr. Weatherby among the lumber, giving a man wearing a blue vest a count of how many pine boards he wanted. Kudzu backed away and scurried close to the base of the shelves, out of the way of the wheels of the rolling baskets. He continued his search for Gatorade, for anything orange.

He found orange gloves, orange fencing, and spools of orange cords, but no orange lightning. None low and none high. In fact, he found very few bottles of anything.

The next time he spotted Mr. Weatherby was where the feed was, and Kudzu felt warm inside for Quincy's future on the farm. If only Kudzu could make peace with Victoria, then there would be total peace. But he knew he was running out of time. Mr. Weatherby's basket was getting full. He would be leaving soon, and Kudzu didn't want to get left behind in a place without friends and acorns.

On his way out, Kudzu double-checked and triple-checked every section and corner and every speck and spot. He didn't know how in the world he would have carried a bottle of Gatorade out of here anyway, but he would have tried. Then, near the entrance, he happened to see someone slide open a door on a box much like the refrigerator in the Weatherbys' home, and inside the box were rows of different-colored bottles. The person pulled out a brown bottle, of course, not an orange bottle. Humans and their mud!

Kudzu waited until the person had stepped away, and then he ran up to the box, and through the foggy glass door he saw what he'd come hoping to find: a bottle with an orange lightning bolt and an orange cap, filled with orange lightning, he guessed. Gatorade at last!

He leaped onto the bottom ledge, quickly pried his claws around the edge of the door, and pulled on it as if he were trying to move the biggest rock. He really put all his weight and strength into it, and slowly the door gave, and cold air leaked out, swirling around him. Gradually, he pushed the door farther and farther back, then leaned against it and caught his breath.

There it stood beside him, a bottle of Gatorade. Careful to keep his back propped against the door, he reached with his front legs and hugged the top of the bottle, pulling it to him. More and more the bottle tipped toward him, until it finally fell over and landed on his toes.

"Eeeooooo!" screamed Kudzu. He hopped up in pain, and when he did that, the door slid shut behind him.

"Uh, oh," said Kudzu, speaking aloud as if the bottles in the cold bottle box could hear him and, like an army of ants, rush to rescue him. He climbed over the over-turned Gatorade and tried to open the door, but from this side he couldn't slip his claws around the edge of the door. Surely, someone would come by any second and want their cold bottle of mud! Surely, before he froze!

He looked at the glass but couldn't see through it, so with his paw he wiped the fog away, and he was surprised to see Mr. Weatherby reaching for the door.

Kudzu ducked behind the nearest bottle of mud just in time before Mr. Weatherby pulled the door open.

"Let's see," Mr. Weatherby muttered to himself. "One for me," he said, wrapping his hand around a green bottle and pulling it out, "and one for Mama," he said, his hand clutching the bottle of mud Kudzu happened to be hiding behind.

Kudzu squeezed his eyes nearly closed as if the moment would be less embarrassing if he saw less of it. That didn't work. At the sight of Kudzu, Mr. Weatherby's eyes grew as wide as the orange caps on Gatorade bottles.

"What in tarnation!" said Mr. Weatherby.

Kudzu grinned at him, showing him his big nut-cracking front teeth. Since he was already caught, he decided to make the most of the situation. He bent down behind the Gatorade bottle and shoved it out of the box, then hopped down after it.

Mr. Weatherby let the cooler door go and stood motionless as he watched Kudzu use his nose to roll the bottle of orange Gatorade down the center aisle of the store and out the automatic doors. Mr. Weatherby stepped away from his basket and watched Kudzu roll the bottle all the way to the truck, his orange tail flashing behind him in the sunlight almost like lightning itself. That was when Quincy hopped over the tailgate, picked the bottle up in his mouth, and hopped back in the truck.

"Is this all for you, sir?" a cashier asked him. "If you're ready to check out, I can help you."

Mr. Weatherby walked over without a word and emptied

his hands of his Sprite and Coke. "I'm also buying a Gatorade, I guess. It's already outside," he said, pointing toward the doors. He craned his head to take another look outside, and through the glass he saw Kudzu sitting like before on Quincy's back—as if everything Mr. Weatherby had just witnessed had never happened.

CHAPTER 16

A Season for Dreams

Mr. Weatherby returned to his truck with the most magical object either Kudzu or Quincy had ever laid eyes on. There was nothing in the rolling basket Kudzu hadn't already seen inside the store—the pine boards, the tar shingles, the box of nails, the enormous bag of feed. But what floated above the basket and above Mr. Weatherby's head, the apple on a string, must have come from an invisible secret place, as if pulled from deep within Mr. Weatherby himself. As if one of Mrs. Weatherby's red spring-time tulips had somehow sprouted from his chest on the most fragile of stems and was bobbing with the breeze. Kudzu and Quincy stared in amazement, speechless and barkless alike.

Because Mr. Weatherby had wanted to be prepared with dog food for as long as possible, he'd bought the largest bag there was, which was actually on sale and came with a balloon. He hadn't owned a dog in years. He and Mrs. Weatherby had thought that someday they would buy one, though a small one that could sit in their laps like their cat, Dollop, but it was good to be reminded that sometimes you can't choose whom you'll take into your home and will love. It's better to have an open heart and let it fly where the wind wants to take it—like this apple-colored balloon, Mr. Weatherby thought.

Quincy and Kudzu stood by and watched, wagging their

tails, as Mr. Weatherby loaded his supplies into the back of the truck. When he finished, he closed the gate and dipped his hand into his jacket pocket.

"One for each of you clever rascals," said Mr. Weatherby, and he opened his hand to reveal the two dirt clods the woman in the long white coat had given him earlier at the snake-on-a-stick place.

Without hesitation, Quincy stepped forward and took one from Mr. Weatherby, but Kudzu wasn't so eager. Mr. Weatherby held the dirt clod out for him as far as he could reach his arm over the side of the truck, and Kudzu stretched his neck to sniff it.

"It's okay," said Mr. Weatherby. "It's a treat."

Kudzu liked treats, but the dirt clod didn't smell like dirt. It smelled like a treat, like a meat treat, like a dried-meat treat. So he opened his mouth as wide as he could and took it.

"Thank you," Kudzu mumbled.

"Yeah, thank you!" Quincy said, nearly shouting between bites.

Mr. Weatherby twisted the cap off his bottle of Sprite and watched them for a moment. Then he tied the balloon to his radio antennae and put his basket away.

Kudzu was so busy gnawing on his treat, and Quincy was so busy watching him, already having finished his own much earlier, that they never noticed they were passing Quincy Street or later the kudzu patch. Somehow the long drive had become a short drive, and before they knew it, they were back on the farm.

Mr. Weatherby parked his truck by the porch and got out with the bottle of Coke. "I'll be right back," he told Quincy, or both Kudzu and Quincy, then went up the porch steps and opened the door. "Mama," they heard him call as he shut the door behind him.

Victoria floated up to the balloon and tapped it curiously with the tip of her proboscis. Kudzu and Quincy quietly watched her fly away, then return and circle the balloon twice, before finally appearing before them with a look of amazement on her face.

"What kind of flower may I ask is that?" she asked, and in the same breath, seeing the bottle with the orange lightning bolt and the orange cap in the corner of the truck bed, she cheered, "Gatorade!" She fluttered her wings together so that she seemed to be clapping, and as her wings clapped, she flew straight up. Then, just as suddenly, she stopped clapping and dropped back down. "Oh my, oh my!" she sang. "How a butterfly loves her nectar, her nectar, her sweet Gatorade nectar!"

"My oh my," grinned Kudzu. He'd never seen this side of Victoria.

"Would you please, dear dog," she said, "be so kind as to carry my Gatorade for me?" She smiled and twinkled her enormous eyes, and Quincy, nodding, picked the bottle up in his mouth.

"Right over here, please oh please," she said.

Kudzu held on, and Quincy hopped out of the truck with a jingle of his collar and tag, then followed her to the flowerbed where Kudzu had once lived.

"And will you be so kind as to puncture the bottle with your teeth. Be careful," she instructed Quincy. "Don't bite down too hard. Just enough with those sharp canines you have, that's right, to create a little leak for little me. Ohhhhh," she sang again, clapping her wings again, "perfect!" Then, just as suddenly as before, she stopped clapping and dropped down, though this time all the way down, down to the Gatorade bottle lying on the ground. Her straw-like proboscis plunged with perfect aim into the hole Quincy had made in the bottle. Instantly, like lightning, she was lost to the nectar's sweet taste. Quietly and steadily, she sipped and sipped and sipped some more.

Quincy grinned. "I'm glad we got it for her."

"No kidding!" said Kudzu.

A whistling tune coming from the garage turned their heads and perked up their ears. Owen ran out of the garage in the direction of the truck, and walking a few steps behind him was Mr. Weatherby, carrying tools that he used to cut down trees and to pound boards together. He was whistling but was not whistling at anyone in particular. He was simply whistling, as a happy mockingbird will whistle throughout the day, as he returned to his truck.

Owen stood at the fender where the balloon was tied to the radio antennae, and he stretched his arms upward as if he might reach it.

"I'll get it for you," Mr. Weatherby said but passed Owen to set his tools in the back of the truck.

Owen moaned.

"I thought you might like that balloon," Mr. Weatherby said. "Can you say *balloon*?"

"Ooon," smiled Owen.

"That's right," smiled Mr. Weatherby.

Mr. Weatherby stepped up to the antennae and untied the string. "Here you go," he said, and he tied the string to the boy's wrist. "I need your help now. Come with me," he told Owen. He took his free hand and led Owen to the passenger side and strapped him in.

Instead of hopping back in, Quincy trotted behind the truck as Mr. Weatherby drove slowly to the chicken yard and parked.

Mr. Weatherby patted Quincy on the head, then gave a good look at his farm from this location—up the sloping land at the flower-surrounded house, which wasn't close but wasn't far away either, and at the pecan trees and the persimmon trees, which were closer, and at the chicken yard, which would finally be well protected. "What do you think, boy?" he asked. "Isn't this a nice spot for your house?"

"What do you think, Kudzu?" asked Quincy.

"Of course, it is," said Kudzu.

Quincy thought so, too. He wagged his tail.

"All right, then," said Mr. Weatherby, beginning to unload his supplies, while Owen ran in circles, tugging the balloon and letting it rise.

All day long Quincy stayed nearby and watched Mr. Weatherby build a new house for him. Owen would help him sometimes, but most of the time he played with Quincy. He'd hold the balloon out to him, and Quincy would bump it with his nose to make the cute boy laugh. Whenever Mr. Weatherby paused in his sawing and hammering, he would speak to Owen or Quincy and praise them, telling them how good and smart they were, and he'd step away to give them a pat on the head.

While Mr. Weatherby worked, Kudzu worked. Kudzu was building his own house, right next to Quincy's. And when Kudzu had completed his new burrow, he rested beside Quincy and watched Owen try to put the finishing touch on Quincy's house. At first, though, no one understood what Owen was trying to do. He appeared to be trying to climb onto the roof of Quincy's house. He stood beside the house and reached upward with his balloon.

"You want on top?" Mr. Weatherby asked, but Owen said, "No, *oon. Oon.*"

Mr. Weatherby grinned. "You want the balloon on top?"

"Uh-huh," said Owen.

Mr. Weatherby nodded. "All right, little man," he said and untied the floating apple from Owen's wrist and tied it to a nail on the doghouse so that it would fly high above, announcing to everyone on the farm that this was Quincy's house. This was Quincy's new home!

Still, something worried Mr. Weatherby, and he was troubled throughout his dinner and for the rest of the night. What name should he give his dog? He wanted a name that suggested strength and intelligence, but one that also captured

the lovable side of his dog's personality. Mrs. Weatherby liked a cute name, and Dollop was a cute name for a cute cat. But Mr. Weatherby needed to go in a different direction with their dog. He wanted a human name, but which one?

Mr. Weatherby turned in his sleep all through the night. But he wasn't the only one. Kudzu had also found it difficult to sleep. For the first time in almost a week, he had a bed beneath the ground, and for the first time in his life, he felt trapped in such a place, with nothing but dirt walls on every side. Feeling too lonely to sleep, Kudzu climbed from his new burrow to join Quincy in his new house.

Before Kudzu had a chance to knock on the frame of Quincy's open doorway and announce himself, he heard the nearby sound of a small herd of animals slowly nosing through the grass. He turned and saw what looked like fallen moons scattered in a line on the ground—the faces of Ophelia and her children following her!

Kudzu waved. "Hi there!" he said.

"Hi, Kudzu!" said Ophelia.

"Hey, it's Kudzu!" said one of her children.

"Hey, Kudzu!" said another.

"Hey, Kudzu!" said another.

"Hey, Kudzu!" said another.

"Hey, Kudzu!" said another.

"Hey, Kudzu!" said the last.

Kudzu laughed. "Hey, everybody!" he said.

Then from behind him, a much lower voice said, "Hey, Kudzu!"

Kudzu turned around to see Quincy standing in the doorway of his house. "Hey, Quincy!" said Kudzu.

"Hi, Quincy!" said Ophelia.

"Hey, Quincy!" said one of her children.

"Hey, Quincy!" said another.

"Hey, Quincy!" said another.

"Hey, Quincy!" said another.

"Hey, Quincy!" said another.

"Hey, Quincy!" said the last.

Ophelia chuckled at the good spirits of her children and their growing memory. They hadn't forgotten the scent of friends. She turned a smile to Quincy and gave him two thumbs up. "Congratulations on your new home! Everyone on the farm is talking about it."

Quincy wagged his tail, and it thumped the walls of his house. "Thanks!" he said. "It's what I've always wanted."

"We come by here every night, so we'll stop by and say hello every night," she said.

"Please do," Quincy said. "Y'all are always welcome."

Kudzu looked up at Quincy. He was glad that during the winter months his friend wouldn't be alone at the loneliest times of the night.

Together in the doorway, after watching the opossum family wander away for food in the direction of the persimmon trees, Kudzu and Quincy went inside to lie down for sleep. Quincy hadn't been able to sleep yet tonight either, but now, with Kudzu curled up by his side once again, he could close his eyes and keep them closed. And for the rest of the night and early morning, even long after the rooster crowed at dawn, he slept in perfect peace. As did Kudzu.

Unlike Kudzu and Quincy, however, Mr. Weatherby

opened his eyes as soon as the rooster crowed, and immediately he began considering more dog names. "Arnold?" he asked himself. "Henry? Gary? David? Sammy?" No, he didn't like any of these names for his dog.

Careful not to wake his wife, who was unusually sleepy this morning, he left the bed to put on his robe and slippers, and to put in his teeth. Maybe coffee would warm him up and help him think clearly so that he could come up with the perfect name his dog deserved. Dollop meowed at him as he eased from the bedroom to make a pot of coffee, but he stopped before he reached the kitchen. In the living room, Mr. Weatherby found an encyclopedia lying on the floor as randomly as one of Owen's toys. How could Mrs. Weatherby have dropped it there by mistake and not have heard it fall? He didn't even remember his wife reading any book last night. But here it was, and it appeared to have been placed on the floor on purpose for him to find. The book was left open, and the words faced his direction.

He bent down, picked up the book, and carried it with him to the kitchen table, where he read the articles on the pages that the book had been turned to. He had no idea why his wife would be interested in reading about a city in Illinois that was located on the banks of the Mississippi River. Or about a city in Massachusetts of the very same name, which had received its name from the sixth president of the United States, who had been born there. Or about a college, again of the same name. And that name was *Quincy*. Quincy, Illinois. Quincy, Massachusetts. And Quincy College.

Mr. Weatherby shut the book that Stanley had set out for him to find, and then it struck Mr. Weatherby—*Quincy* was a fine name. As president, John Quincy Adams had shown enormous strength and intelligence. And the name didn't sound too strong or too smart for Mr. Weatherby's lovable pet. The name had a warm, musical quality about it that reminded Mr. Weatherby of a flowing river. Perhaps the Mississippi

River itself, which had once flowed right over this land hundreds of years ago.

Mr. Weatherby repeated the name to himself, and the more he heard it, the more he wanted to sing it out loud. *Quincy, Quincy, Quincy!* he thought. Yes, he decided, that was the name he'd been hoping for all along. It was a name that fit only his dog, and no one else's.

Deciding to put the name to the test, Mr. Weatherby stood up and stepped outside. He didn't want to sing the name in such a way that any dog would come. And he didn't want to shout the name, which might scare the dog into not coming. He chose instead to say the word simply loud enough for the dog to hear, and he would say it only once.

"Quincy," he said, as plainly as he could, and amazing him, Quincy immediately came running.

From then on, that would be the way Mr. Weatherby and Quincy would begin each day. But instead of saying Quincy's name, Mr. Weatherby would always sing his name, and then Quincy would always come running. That was how they began each and every day—until the seasons changed.

In the coldest days of winter, long after Owen had gone back to his own home, Quincy would be allowed to sleep inside the house on a blanket by the kitchen door. And although Quincy liked sleeping in the house, getting more attention from the Weatherbys and getting to visit with Stanley and Dollop, he never hoped it would get that cold ever again. In fact, he always hoped and prayed that the days would soon turn warm. At night, his dreams were always the same. Always of spring.

Quincy would often spend his days lying in wait for spring at the entrance to Kudzu's burrow—even after the entrance had been plugged up with leaves and frost. Somewhere safe in the ground below, in a place Quincy could only dream about, Kudzu was sleeping in a nest of Quincy's own fur. Kudzu had combed out enough fur from Quincy's thick coat to keep him warm all winter long, and the image of that warmed Quincy for just as long.

Eventually, the ground would soften and split open with life, and Quincy would be there when it happened. Eventually, like a flower, Kudzu would rise from his deep slumber and need to fill his belly and stretch his legs to the sun, and to the rainbows between spring showers. Eventually, Kudzu would need to see his old friend Quincy again and tell him how much he had been missed. And Quincy would be there on that day waiting for him. Yes, he would be there, so he could tell his dear, old friend Kudzu the same.

Acknowledgments

Thank you, Julia and A.N. Hall, my mother and stepfather. A.N. inspired this book with a story he told me one day on the small Mississippi farm where they were living, in essence like the Weatherbys. For the same reason that appears in the book, he had set a trap for a chipmunk who lived beneath my mother's flowers. Because art mirrors life (more than we can ever know), you, dear readers, are correct to imagine what happened next. Yes, that happened as well. And then the stray dog that had been coming around their house had done so again in the nick of time, while my stepfather was retrieving his hoe. At the conclusion of his story, my stepfather glanced away with a smile. It was just the two of us standing outside where it all had taken place. We were near the flowerbed, where the yard began to slope and the enormous oak trees around us shimmered from an imperceptible breeze. "What do you know!" he then said. "That chipmunk's mortal enemy set it free." It was at that very moment, with my stepfather's words leaving their impressions on my imagination, I knew my own story, this story, was just beginning.

Thank you, Quincy, for being so Quincy.

Thank you, Dawn Eubanks and Julie Sanford, for reading the first version of this book so many years ago to your young children as well as giving it to your older children to read themselves. I thank you and I thank them for that commitment, and for the animated praise and encouragement that have forever followed.

Thank you, Patricia "Dollop" Collins and Stanley "House Mouse" Thompson, for inspiring characters, for reading the book to Conner, and for generously volunteering to share a later version of this book on multiple occasions with your students at George County Middle School and Central Elementary in Lucedale. The sweet, earnest feedback I received from your students sufficiently demonstrated that this book is ideal for middle-grade readers of all skill levels—and for how that reassurance strengthened my resolve to pursue publication, I am most grateful.

Thank you, Dalen Raymond, for lending me your expertise as an award-winning Montessori teacher and consultant, with nearly forty years of K-6 teaching, by reading and assessing the final version of *Kudzu's Enormous New Life*, and for assuring me that its life lessons make it "a much-needed story for all children today."

Thank you, Sara, for always believing in me as a middle-grade author, for always gently nudging me in the right direction on every decision, and for always smiling at any mention of Kudzu.

Thank you, Emme, for teaching me more about children and children's books than anyone. Your advice hit me the hardest and hit me best. When my book of poems that is dedicated to you came out, you wisely said to me, "Now you need to write a book about Owen."

Lastly, naturally, most importantly, thank you, Owen, for being so you, the final ingredient—the child this book long needed (Mommy and I needed to make you first, for us, before I could truly understand why). Your heart and mind are vast, mysterious, and rich as continents, but they are sound. I hope for those reasons you receive what you deserve: a large following of Owen fans—those many kindred spirits on the spectrum who, because of you, Owen, have never felt alone or too different because you were always there with them as a warm part of their childhood.

About Atmosphere Press

Atmosphere Press is an independent, full-service publisher for excellent books in all genres and for all audiences. Learn more about what we do at atmospherepress.com.

We encourage you to check out some of Atmosphere's latest releases, which are available at Amazon.com and via order from your local bookstore:

Do Lions Cry?, by Erina White
Sadie and Charley Finding Their Way, by Bonnie Griesemer
Silly Sam and the Invisible Jinni, by Shayla Emran Bajalia
Feeling My Feelings, by Shilpi Mahajan
Zombie Mombie Saves the Day, by Kelly Lucero
The Fable King, by Sarah Philpot
Blue Goggles for Lizzy, by Amanda Cumbey
Neville and the Adventure to Cricket Creek, by Juliana Houston
Peculiar Pets: A Collection of Exotic and Quixotic Animal Poems, by Kerry Cramer
Carlito the Bat Learns to Trick-or-Treat, by Michele Lizet Flores
Zoo Dance Party, by Joshua Mutters
Beau Wants to Know, a picture book by Brian Sullivan

About the Author

Sidney Thompson is the author of *Follow the Angels, Follow the Doves: The Bass Reeves Trilogy, Book One* (2020) and *Hell on the Border: The Bass Reeves Trilogy, Book Two* (2021), award-winning historical novels that narrate the real-life story of a slave who fought his master, a prominent politician and officer in the 11th Texas Cavalry Regiment, for his freedom and later became the greatest lawman of the American Wild West. Thompson is currently at work on the third novel of the trilogy. He holds a Ph.D. in American literature/African American narratives and an M.F.A. in creative writing. Thompson's other books include *You/Wee: Poems from a Father* (2018) and *Sideshow: Stories* (2006), winner of Foreword INDIES Silver Award for Short Story Collection of the Year. Thompson teaches creative writing and African American literature at Texas Christian University in Fort Worth. He and his wife, Sara, have four children: Shania, Josh, Emme, and Owen.

You can follow the author @sidneythompsonauthor on Instagram, @authorsidneythompson on Facebook, and @sidneythompson1 on Twitter.